PAPOOSED

An Essie Cobb Senior Sleuth Mystery

by

Patricia Rockwell

This book is fiction. All characters, events, and organizations portrayed in this novel are the product of the author's imagination or are used fictitiously. Any resemblance to actual persons—living or dead—is entirely coincidental.

Copyright © 2012 by Patricia Rockwell

All rights reserved. No parts of this book may be reproduced or transmitted in any form or by any means, electronic or mechanical, including photocopying, recording or by any information storage and retrieval system, without written permission from the author, except for the inclusion of brief quotations in a review.

For information, email **Cozy Cat Press**, cozycatpress@aol.com or visit our website at: www.cozycatpress.com

COZY CAT PRESS

ISBN: 978-0-9848402-1-2
Printed in the United States of America

Cover design by Atomic Werewolf Studio, www.atomicwerewolfstudio.com

Dedicated to all the wonderful senior citizens at Independence Village in Naperville, Illinois. Thank you for your inspiration.

Chapter One
"Every child begins the world again."
–Henry David Thoreau

"Someone is trying to sabotage me," Essie thought she heard the young waiter say. Something about wanting her help. In the kitchen. Was the man being threatened by one of the kitchen workers at Happy Haven? Surely not. She sat at her table pondering his whispered remark as Santos, the young waiter, slipped back into the kitchen after neatly depositing hot fudge sundaes in front of Essie and her three dinner companions–Opal, Marjorie, and Fay. A sprig of holly provided a festive holiday touch to the top of each dessert.

"What was that about, Essie?" asked Opal, on her right, her stern eyes glaring over her glasses at Essie from her imposing height. Opal obviously didn't approve of anyone making small talk with the staff.

"Santos was just asking my opinion," fibbed Essie. No need to drag her three gal pals into this little mystery until she knew exactly what Santos was talking about.

"He was whispering in your ear," added Marjorie on her left, with a sprightly wiggle of her shoulders. The white fur collar on Marjorie's red wool sweater made her look like one of Santa's helpers. "It seemed rather cozy to me, Essie!"

"Oh, for St. Nicholas' sake!" cried Essie, keeping with the Christmas spirit, "He was asking my opinion about something."

"What?" demanded Opal in a whisper, leaning in towards Essie with a superior glare.

"Opal," snapped Essie, plopping her red napkin down next to her now melting sundae. "He's just a nice young man who values the advice of a more experienced person—such as myself."

"But what kind of experience does he need?" asked Marjorie, in a suggestive whisper.

"Marjorie! He's young enough to be my grandson!" retorted Essie, grabbing her spoon and scooping up a huge mound of chocolate sauce and ice cream and ramming it into her mouth, thus effectively ending any further conversation for the moment–at least from her end. The fourth member of the group–Fay–sitting across from Essie, gobbled her sundae without comment.

All four women became suddenly silent as they concentrated on finishing their sundaes before the ice cream had melted away to a soupy mess. It was really too cold to eat ice cream any way, reasoned Essie, being only a few weeks before Christmas. By the time Essie had sipped the last few spoonsful of ice cream, the women's focus had changed–Santos, the waiter, and his whispered request, apparently forgotten.

"Oh, look," whispered Opal, staring above Essie's head and giving her a little shove with her elbow.

"Hubert Darby's suspenders are falling off again! Will that man ever learn to keep his pants up?"

"Where?" demanded Marjorie, quickly turning her head of curly reddish-silver locks toward the direction that Opal's elbow indicated. "Oh, my! You're right! Look! When he bends over to pick up his tray, you can see his crack!"

"Marjorie!" exclaimed Opal.

"You've heard worse, Opal!" countered the former elementary school teacher. "First graders say 'butt crack' all the time! It's one of their favorite insults!"

"We're not first graders!" responded the sour Opal with a dramatic sniff. Opal's years as an administrative assistant for a major legal firm were evident in her professional and stern demeanor.

"Stop it, you two!" said Essie, extending her arms and patting the hands of her friends who sat to either side of her at the small square table, charmingly decorated with a glowing red candle surrounded by small poinsettias. "The poor man probably doesn't have a clue that his suspenders are lop-sided and . . . ."

"And his pants are falling down!" added Marjorie with a devious smile. "That's fine with me, Essie! More men should wear suspenders and then maybe more pants would drop!"

"Marjorie, you're disgusting!" said Opal, posture perfect, fingering the cameo around her neck with a prim haughtiness.

"I'm sure his suspenders will do their job," said Essie, continuing to pat her friends' arms, the patting becoming more insistent as Opal and Marjorie bent over Essie scowling at each other. "Stop it, now! Both of you! Hubert Darby doesn't deserve this kind of treatment from either of you."

The two women finally shrugged and leaned back in their chairs. When Essie, the leader of their group, gave orders—no matter how thinly veiled—the other three women typically followed them. At least, that was what had happened recently. Essie had gotten riled up when one of the Happy Haven residents had fallen into a coma after winning a dollar playing Bingo and had sent all four of them on a merry adventure to discover a possible mystery behind the event. As it turned out, the man had recovered and the mystery was solved, but Essie and her three henchmen—or rather henchwomen—had played a major part in bringing it to a positive conclusion.

Opal and Marjorie glanced at Essie. Essie wasn't much different than they were—all senior citizens living in the Happy Haven Assisted Living Facility. Essie was the oldest at ninety, but Marjorie, Opal, and Fay were close behind her in their mid-eighties. Of course, everyone who lived at Happy Haven was a senior citizen, but Essie, Opal, Marjorie, and Fay were a close-knit group primarily because they always sat together for their meals. Indeed, everyone at Happy Haven had a regular seat at an assigned table for all meals—breakfast, lunch, and dinner— so tablemates got to know each other quite well.

"Gone!" exclaimed the fourth member of the group sitting across from Essie in her wheelchair. The pudgy little woman examined her spoon in obvious frustration that the ice cream and chocolate sauce in her dish had vanished.

"You ate it all, Fay!" said Essie, leaning across the table to the small lady, who was now trying to scrape the sides of the dish of any possible remaining dessert.

"I guess she liked it," noted Marjorie, smiling warmly at Fay. Fay continued to manipulate the spoon against the sundae dish with no success in securing any additional sauce to eat.

"It's good there's something she can get excited about," offered Opal with a wise sigh.

"How true!" added Essie. "I don't often know what she's thinking. When she makes a comment I sometimes get a little glimpse of what's going on in there." Essie smiled at Opal and Marjorie and nodded at their fourth member. An outside observer might conclude that Fay was slow because of her inability or unwillingness to communicate fully. They would be wrong, as all three of her friends knew well. In previous adventures, the women had discovered that although Fay was not terribly talkative, she had abilities that none of the rest of them possessed. Each day, it seemed, they discovered something new about Fay. They knew, for instance, that Fay was a computer whiz. They didn't know how Fay had developed her skills, but they surmised that she had learned them either in her previous job as a research librarian or from one of her children. They were also not at all certain what had caused Fay's present rather uncommunicative state, but they loved her just the same and all three adjusted their own schedules when needed to help Fay function at Happy Haven. It had become obvious to them that Fay was capable of saying almost anything, but that she just saved her comments for the most appropriate–or sometimes–inappropriate– moments.

"Hello, Miss Essie!" said a male voice.

The women all turned at once in the direction of the sound. Standing beside Essie was the very man whom they had all been deriding because of his unhooked suspenders and low-slung trousers. The man was large, tall and dressed rather nattily, if you ignored the obviously open suspender on the back of his pants. His hands were twisting painfully in the pockets of his bright red cardigan vest that featured Christmas reindeer on the front. His large round head was ringed with a halo of thin, straight brownish-grey fringe. A bright red tie set off his light blue shirt and matched the suspenders which were attached to his khaki trousers. A nice pair of clean black and white sneakers completed his ensemble. The man blushed noticeably and repeated his greeting in a low grumbly voice.

"Hello, Miss Essie."

"Uh, Hubert," said Essie with a weak smile at the man and a concerned glance back at her three friends.

"You look nice today, Miss Essie," said Hubert Darby, rocking back and forth on his rubber-soled shoes with a sort of controlled frenzy. Essie bit her lip.

"Thank you, Hubert," she replied. She again glanced at her friends who remained frozen, waiting for the continuation of the conversation. It appeared that Hubert Darby did not intend to speak to the other women at the table. "Hubert? You know my tablemates—Opal, Marjorie, and Fay?"

"Um," he grumbled, or maybe moaned. "Miss Essie, you . . . you . . . ." He continued looking at Essie, attempting to form his sentence, rocking on his feet, his face getting progressively redder. Essie thought that if it got much redder, the man's head might just explode. She continued to smile at him politely awaiting his next statement. Essie believed in being patient when someone was having difficulty speaking and obviously Hubert Darby was having difficulty. It was somewhat like what happened to Fay, reasoned Essie, but when Fay spoke, she didn't have any trouble saying whatever she wanted to say, she just didn't say very much very often. All of a sudden, the man turned abruptly and scurried away from the table and out of the dining hall, his trousers drooping in back because they were held up by just one suspender.

"He has a crush on you, Essie!" said Marjorie with a wink.

"Just what she needs," added Opal with a sympathetic sigh.

"Don't be ridiculous," replied Essie. "He was just making polite conversation. I try to encourage him because he obviously has trouble speaking."

"Oh, it's more than that, Essie," said Marjorie, "Hubert is smitten with you! He wore his red suspenders! Probably because he planned to plight his troth."

"He should have made certain they were hooked to his pants," noted Opal smugly, "before he went courting."

"Hubert Darby is not smitten with me," said Essie firmly. Fay had given up on her empty ice cream bowl and had fallen asleep in her wheelchair. "I'm just someone he trusts."

"It's more than that, Essie," added Marjorie, with a jab at Essie's shoulder. "You'll see! I know the signs. I used to see this kind of behavior in many a love-struck first-grade boy when I taught elementary school."

Before Essie could respond or even digest Marjorie's evaluation of Hubert Darby's unusual pronouncement, Santos, the young Hispanic waiter, had returned and was standing beside Essie.

"Miss Essie," whispered the waiter, bending down and speaking quietly into Essie's ear. "Miss Essie, can you come back to the kitchen now?"

"Santos," replied Essie, looking up into the frightened face of the young man who bussed her table several meals a day. "What's wrong?"

"Miss Essie," he repeated softly but insistently in her ear, "por favor. I cannot talk about it here. You come back to kitchen. I show you."

"Show me?"

"Por favor! Please!"

As her gal pals looked on incredulously, Essie rose and grabbed her red and black walker which was parked next to her chair and followed the young man through the bustling dining room and into the kitchen. Santos moved quickly, turning his head back every moment or so to be certain that Essie was behind him. She was. Although Essie was ninety and unable to walk upright on her own, when driving her walker she was hell on wheels and could go faster than most people could walk.

"This way, Miss Essie," called out Santos, as he wound his way through the main kitchen area. The many workers barely glanced at their co-worker followed by one of the Happy Haven residents as they attended to their business of washing plates, preparing dishes for future meals, inventorying supplies, and other tasks. Santos led Essie quickly through a back hallway where the hubbub of the kitchen lessened. She followed him down a long hallway stacked with boxes of goods. Some boxes were opened. One box held giant cans of peaches. Santos continued quickly down the hallway. Essie could see a closet door at the end of it. It was obvious that Santos was taking her to this closet to show her something, but what, she had no idea. Maybe, he wants my opinion on what type of vegetable or fruit to serve for an upcoming meal? No, that doesn't make sense, she thought. The kitchen staff never asked residents for their input on meals. They certainly wouldn't ask just one resident for her opinion. Santos finally reached the door which was open a crack. He turned to Essie who had arrived behind him. He looked over her head, as if to see if anyone was around or watching. Then he carefully opened the closet door.

Inside, Essie could see a walk-in storage area. A change in air pressure indicated to her that the storage closet was noticeably warmer than the hallway. As they moved inside, she saw that shelving units lined the three walls. On all shelves were boxes of packaged foods and canned goods. Santos moved quickly to the far end of the closet and bent down to the lowest shelf. Essie could see an open cardboard box full of what looked like thin white towels. Santos knelt beside the box and gently lifted the towels. Essie peered into the box. Inside, sleeping soundly was a totally beautiful–totally round and chubby–newborn baby.

Chapter Two
"Babies are always more trouble than you thought–and more wonderful."
–Charles Osgood

"Santos!" exclaimed Essie, her eyes agog. "That's a baby!"

"Madre Dios, Miss Essie!" whispered Santos, rising and putting his hand gently but firmly in front of Essie's mouth. "Quiet, por favor. Baby sleep. No one can know."

"You mean, no one on the staff knows there's a baby here? Don't they come back here for supplies?" Now Essie had her hands on her hips as she scowled at the young man incredulously.

"Oh, no!" he continued in a soft voice very close to Essie's face. "Baby is secret! I hide him before dinner, before crew get here."

"But, why, Santos?" asked Essie, glancing back and forth between Santos and the infant peacefully sleeping in the box on the lower shelf. "What are you doing with a baby in this storage closet? Oh, my! Is this your baby?"

"Oh, no, Miss Essie!" cried Santos with a certain amount of shock. "Not my baby! I not married!"

"Of course, I didn't mean . . ." Essie sputtered, "I meant, maybe the baby of some woman you were . . .

um . . . dating?" She cringed as she looked to see how Santos would respond to her delicate phraseology.

"No! No!" continued Santos, "This is Maria's baby, Miss Essie. Maria work here. I get Maria job in kitchen several months ago. I did not know about baby then."

"What?" replied Essie. "This is . . . confusing, Santos! What is going on? And why did you drag me back here to see this poor child? Where is its mother?"

"That is big problem, Miss Essie," said Santos, his voice rising along with his shoulders. "I don't know where Maria is."

"You don't know where the baby's mother is?" she questioned. "How can that be? I thought you said she worked here. So, where is she?"

"She's gone, Miss Essie!"

"Gone where?"

"I do not know, Miss Essie!" replied the young man, shaking his head pitifully. "Oh, Miss Essie, I do not know what to do. Can you help me?" With a miserable face, he looked at the old woman and slowly sunk to the floor in a heap next to the baby in the box.

"Me?" snorted Essie. "What do you expect me to do? I don't know where this child's mother has gone."

"I know, Miss Essie," said Santos from the floor, his head in his hands. Essie tapped her foot. This was obviously a very serious situation. A newborn child needed its mother. It didn't need to be hidden away in a closet among the canned green beans. Essie sighed and looked around frantically as if she'd find the answer to this dilemma in the labels on the canned fruit. Finally, she twirled her walker around and sat down on the built-in leather seat.

"Now, start from the beginning, young man," she ordered, "and start now."

"Yes, Miss Essie," replied Santos still on the ground, cringing as Essie shook her finger in his direction. "I do not even know Maria is pregnant."

"When was this?"

"Maria? I do not know about baby when Maria and Gerald move here six months ago."

"Wait a minute," said Essie, holding out the palm of her hand. "Who's this Gerald?"

"Gerald is Maria's husband. They meet in Mexico. Gerald is American. He meet Maria in Los Colinas Rojas . . . where Maria lives. Maria and Gerald, they get married. Very fast! That very bad, says mi madre . . . my mother. She says very bad when man and woman get married too soon . . . and . . . ."

"I get it, Santos," said Essie, motioning for him to speed up his tale.

"Maria, she make very bad mistake. She marry Gerald too fast. She not think first. Maria and Gerald move to America. Mi madre . . . my mother . . . says you cannot trust American man . . . ." Santos was gesturing wildly as he sat cross-legged on the concrete floor, telling his story.

"Yes, yes," said Essie, nodding, "American men are the scum of the earth. What happened? Obviously, nothing good or this little baby would not be . . . ."

"Oh, Maria is very happy in America, Miss Essie," said Santos with a smile. "She and husband move here to Reardon. Maria get job here at Happy Haven. Now I have friend from Mexico I can speak to here in America. But Maria, she does not speak English good like me!" The young waiter puffed out his chest proudly and wiped his hands on his apron.

"Yes, yes, Santos," said Essie, waving her hands more furiously, "but obviously something went wrong."

"Gerald, he does not want Maria to get pregnant," announced Santos sadly.

"What did he expect?" asked Essie, her eyes bulging. "He married her, right?"

"Si, Miss Essie," said Santos, nodding, "but Gerald does not understand Maria's family way. He wants her to use . . . how you say? Control de la Natalidad? The control of birth?"

"Enough information, Santos!" exclaimed Essie, leaning back in her walker, hands to ears.

"Gerald is very good husband until Maria gets pregnant," said Santos tentatively, "then he is very bad husband." Santos looked at the ground forlornly. He dropped his head between his knees and rubbed his temples.

"How?" Essie asked. There was obviously much more to this story than Santos was probably able–or maybe even–willing–to tell her. Finally, the young man took a deep breath.

"He beat Maria," whispered Santos sadly. "He beat her when she tells him she is going to have baby. He tells her to get rid of baby, but Maria, she cannot do that. Maria's family, they do not believe in getting rid of babies. Babies are all very good, even many, many babies. Gerald beats Maria more. Maria tells me about her husband. She tells me her husband beats her all the time. She puts away some money . . . little by little. Maria, she wants to leave husband when baby comes, but she needs money."

"That was very nice of you, Santos, to listen to her," noted Essie. "So where is she? Why is this poor child now in the bottom of a box in this closet?"

"I do not know, Miss Essie," bawled Santos, an actual tear welling up in his eye. "Maria have baby a little bit ago at home. Gerald, he do not take Maria to hospital . . . and Maria, she does not have money, for . . . how you say? Seguro de salud? Insurance?"

"Oh galloping galoshes! She gave birth at home?"

"In her apartment, si."

"I suppose the no-good Gerald didn't help."

"No. Gerald, he is at work. When Gerald comes home, he is very mad. Maria is very scared. Maria, she calls me. She wants to take baby and leave husband. I try to call her every day after baby is born but Maria does not answer, Miss Essie. I am very worried. Tonight Maria comes to work for dinner shift. I think, this is good. Maria, she is okay. Gerald may be okay with baby. Then Maria takes me to closet–this one here." He looked around the tiny room with a pitiful remorseful sigh. "When we come in closet, Maria opens her coat and shows baby to me. I am very worried. Baby is very new. Maria is very weak. Maria has . . .how you say? Contusión?"

"Bruise?"

"Si! Bruise on her face, Miss Essie. I do not know what to do. I do not know why she comes to work tonight."

"So what happened?" asked Essie, now completely engrossed in the young man's tale.

"Maria, she says she is leaving Gerald. She says Gerald beats her and baby."

"Oh no!" exclaimed Essie. "The baby too! How horrible!"

"I know, Miss Essie," agreed Santos. He hopped to his knees. "Maria says she has a plan. Plan to leave husband and protect baby. Maria asks me to watch baby for her until she comes back. Maria says this to me three hours ago, Miss Essie. She is not back yet."

"Not yet?" cried Essie. "Can you call her? Do you have her number?"

"I have only the telephone number for Maria's apartment . . . where she lives with Gerald."

"No, uh cell telephone?" asked Essie. Although Essie didn't herself possess one of these new-fangled personal communication devices, she did realize that many people owned them and that they could come in handy in unusual predicaments—just like this one. Indeed, both of her daughters—and she assumed her son—used their cell telephones frequently.

"What am I going to do, Miss Essie? What if Maria does not return?" pleaded Santos. He was clutching Essie's knees as she sat, perplexed, on her walker seat.

"Why don't you take the baby to Violet or one of the staff nurses?" suggested Essie.

"Oh, no!" replied Santos, aghast. "I cannot do that! Maria makes me promise not to tell anyone about Antonio."

"Antonio?"

"The baby!"

"But you just told me about him, Santos!" whispered Essie loudly, slapping the arms of her walker in frustration.

"I think Maria means not to tell anyone who is a . . . a . . ."

"An authority?"

"Si, Miss Essie. That's it! Maria is afraid . . . if important people know about Antonio, they take him and keep him . . . or even more worse . . . give him to Gerald."

"But isn't Maria a citizen? I mean, she married Gerald."

"Yes, Maria is American citizen . . . I think. I am not sure. I do not know law. Maria does not know either. Gerald tells her she cannot keep baby and he can give baby away."

"He can't do that!"

"Are you sure, Miss Essie?" asked Santos. "Maria is very scared of husband. Very scared for baby." He leaned back on his haunches as he stared up at Essie with his big brown eyes.

"Yes, I can see that," mused Essie, hunkering down on her walker seat in thought. "Do you have any idea where she is now?"

"No," said Santos, "She is in very big hurry when she leaves here tonight. Maria empujó . . . uh, shoves . . . baby in my arms and runs out of closet very fast. When she goes, I do not know what to do. I make little crib for Antonio with the empty box and the old dish towels. When Maria does not come back, I think I will ask Miss Essie. Everyone knows Miss Essie helps Senor Bob when he is in coma. You help him. Senor Bob has big problem just like baby Antonio. You help baby Antonio too, Miss Essie." He looked at her with helpless eyes. The warmth in the small closet was beginning to feel oppressive . . . even to Essie.

"I don't know, Santos," said Essie with a sigh. "It's one thing to figure out how to help an old man. I have a lot of personal experience with being old. I don't have any idea what to do to help this little baby."

"But you will think of something, Miss Essie!" cried Santos. "I know you can! Please do not make me give baby to the authors!"

"The authorities," corrected Essie gently. "Santos, there's no guarantee that the authorities would automatically give Antonio to his father. I'm sure if you explained what Maria had told you, they'd . . ."

"No, Miss Essie," argued Santos. "Gerald is American citizen. Maria is only citizen because she marry Gerald and . . . if he divorce Maria, Maria is not citizen anymore. Authorities take baby."

"Really?" Essie quizzed the young man. "They can do that?"

"Maria says Gerald will send her back to Mexico and put baby in un hogar de crianza . . ."

"What?"

"Un hogar . . . like a house . . . for babies with no father . . . ."

"A foster home?"

"Si! He will put Antonio in foster home if she does not do what he tells her. If Maria complains, Gerald will beat her. I do not know how to help Maria. I do not want Maria to get beating. I do not want Maria to lose baby."

"Surely, Maria has this all figured out," said Essie finally. "She's probably just been delayed a bit in getting back here. She'll probably show up any minute and tell you what she's decided to do. You did say she left hurriedly. That probably means she has a plan."

"I hope so, Miss Essie," said Santos wearily. "I hope she comes back very soon. I must close up kitchen and check out all the workers. It is my night. Then I must lock kitchen and leave." He pushed back a thick lock of dark hair that had flopped over his forehead.

"And if she's not back before you have to lock up?" asked Essie.

"I . . . I . . . do not know."

"You can't leave a baby here in this closet all night long," said Essie. "You know that."

"I know," replied Santos with a wince.

"Assuming she doesn't return," said Essie gingerly, "can't you take him with you overnight and bring him back with you in the morning? Maybe Maria will contact you someway before then."

"That cannot be, Miss Essie."

"Why not?"

"I live with Senor and Senora Peterson. In their boarding house. I have a bedroom on the second floor. I comparto . . . uh, share . . . a bathroom with Senor and Senora. Senor Peterson is a sick man. Senora Peterson takes care of him. I have to be very quiet. I cannot have a baby in the house."

"You mean you don't have your own apartment?" asked Essie. She had assumed that Santos probably lived alone or shared an apartment with one or more other young persons as did so many people today. As a matter of fact, several of her grandchildren had such living arrangements. Obviously, Santos's finances didn't allow such privacy. She had to admire the young man's frugality–and his concern for his friend Maria and her child. Said child was even now making himself known. As Essie glanced down at the cardboard box on the lower shelf, she could see the dish towel coverlets start to move. An almost inaudible coo emitted from the box.

"Oh, dear!" she moaned. "What can be done?"

"You, Miss Essie!" said Santos with a smile. "You take the baby! Santos knows you good lady, Miss Essie. You will take good care of Antonio. You are all alone in your apartment. Yes, Miss Essie?"

"Yes, I live alone," agreed Essie, "but I can't keep a baby in my apartment. My neighbors would hear it crying. I'd get in trouble with the administration of Happy Haven. Violet would never approve of me . . . or anyone . . . keeping an infant in their room! Besides, I don't have any supplies! I mean, what about food? Diapers? Clothes?"

"Oh, Miss Essie," said Santos, "you are most clever lady I know! You know what to do!" He looked at her and then at the small, tan, round face, now just opening his eyes in the box. Essie scooted her walker closer to the box and peered down at the baby. An ugly gash lined the baby's right cheek and Essie noticed a bruise on one of his fat little legs as he writhed out of his makeshift blankets. Despite his injuries, Antonio looked directly into Essie's face and beamed.

"All right!" she said, with a pitiful sigh. "Give him here! But only tonight!" With that, she rose and lifted the leather seat on her walker. Santos carefully picked up the small bundle, dish towels and all and gently placed him in the wire mesh basket directly under the seat on Essie's walker. Ever so carefully, Essie lowered the seat, being cautious that no toes or fingers were caught between the seat and the basket beneath. Then with a shake of her finger at Santos and a quick warning finger to her lips, she swiftly maneuvered her walker out of the storage closet, through the now empty kitchen, and into the dining hall.

Chapter Three

"Even when freshly washed and relieved of all obvious confections, children tend to be sticky."
–Fran Lebowitz

Essie rolled her walker with her usual expertise, carefully dodging chairs placed around square tables arranged randomly in Happy Haven's large dining hall. She was torn between going her usual super speed so she could get to her room before the baby inside her walker's basket made any noticeable noise, and maintaining a more casual rate so that she didn't accidentally bump into anything and injure or–at a minimum–disturb the little fellow within.

As she passed her own table, she noted that Opal and Marjorie were still seated, sipping their coffee. Fay remained in her wheelchair, snoring gently.

"Essie," called out Marjorie, as Essie whizzed past. "Essie, what happened in the kitchen? What did Santos want?"

"Essie!" yelled Opal to Essie's back as Essie made a sharp turn to the left and headed towards the door. "Essie! Where are you going? What happened?"

The commotion of Essie's entrance from the kitchen and immediate exit–along with the cries of her table companions–awakened the sleeping Fay, who looked around, startled and then reached for her coffee cup when she realized that she was still at the dinner table.

"Sorry, Opal, Marjorie!" Essie cried out over her shoulder as she zoomed past her friends. "Can't talk now!" She made a bee-line down the center of the dining hall towards the main entrance. Opal looked at Marjorie.

"That's strange!" Opal whispered to her shorter tablemate. Fay, now awake, stared at Essie's back as she wheeled down the center aisle of the dining hall.

"Where do you think she's going in such a hurry?" asked Marjorie, still focused on Essie's retreating form in the distance.

"I don't know," replied Opal. "What could that kitchen boy . . . that Santos . . . have shown her to cause her to rush out of here so fast?"

"It's not like her to skip her coffee like this," added Marjorie. At that comment, Fay pressed the button on the arm of her wheelchair that activated the vehicle and quickly guided herself away from the table and through the dining hall.

"Fay!" called out Opal, "where are you going?"

"What's gotten into her now?" Marjorie asked Opal, puzzled. The two women looked at each other and then, at almost the same time, they set down their coffee cups, rose, grabbed their walkers, and rolled quickly out of the dining hall, single file after Fay.

Outside of the dining hall, Essie entered the Happy Haven lobby, the one place where she knew she would be likely to encounter the greatest amount of traffic.

She glanced around quickly and saw only a few residents parked in front of the fireplace enjoying the blazing fire and the Christmas stockings hanging above it. She gave her walker an extra budge over the edge of the carpet, being careful not to jostle the baby inside. Unfortunately, in her haste, one of her wheels became stuck on the carpet edge, something it had done numerous times before. As she bent over to loosen the rubber wheel, a voice above her made her skin crawl. She looked up.

"Essie," said a slender, regal-looking woman with sleek, dark, shoulder-length hair combed strategically behind her ears. "You seem to be in quite a hurry tonight."

"Oh, Miss Hendrickson!" replied Essie, looking up at Happy Haven's imposing Director Violet Hendrickson. Essie continued to manipulate her rubber wheel and eventually got it unstuck from the wayward carpet thread.

"A problem?" continued Violet, arms crossed, tapping a pencil against her elbow. She moved around Essie and stood directly in front of her walker, blocking her way.

"No! No! Miss Hendrickson," explained Essie, "just have to get to the bathroom. You know, too much coffee! I'm ninety! Can't be helped!" With this brief explanation, she ducked around the woman and proceeded on her way, leaving Violet Hendrickson, standing in the center of the lobby, gazing after Essie's retreating form with a look of more than mild curiosity.

Essie knew that Violet was suspicious of her because Essie had stuck her nose into Violet's background and had recently almost cost Violet her job. Although Essie was always exceedingly polite to Violet, Violet appeared to view Essie as a potential trouble-maker. Sometimes Essie wondered if Violet thought she was the director of a home for criminals rather than senior citizens. At least, that's how Essie felt around the dour, humorless woman. Opal and Marjorie thought Essie was imagining things—and well she might be.

Essie continued through the lobby, all decked out in its traditional holiday finery. The central focus was a gigantic two-story tall spruce tree covered from top to bottom with lights and ornaments. At its base, a vintage railroad train careened around small tracks—its tiny whistle announcing its arrival. Still no peep from the baby in the basket, luckily, thought Essie, as she zoomed around the tree towards the family room. She could hear Opal and Marjorie calling behind her from the dining hall. As she glanced back, she saw Fay following her in her motorized wheelchair. Oh, no! she thought, I don't need them involved in this! It's bad enough that I'm involved! She pressed on towards her room which was on the far side of the lobby, past the family room and down the hallway on the right. She was committed now. Hopefully, Opal and Marjorie and Fay would just give up on following her and go on to their own rooms. She couldn't worry about that now. She forged ahead as fast as she was able.

As she turned into her hallway from the family room, she ran smack dab into Hubert Darby. Oh, dear! Why is he down this hallway? He doesn't live in this wing of the building, she recalled. What if he is trying to find me?

"Essie!" exclaimed Hubert, "Hello, Essie!"

She was forced to stop. He was standing directly in front of her.

"Essie," continued Hubert, his suspenders still noticeably unhooked she noticed, "I . . . I dropped by your room."

"That's nice of you, Hubert," said Essie, then . . . with a quick maneuver to her left, she whizzed around Hubert, yelling back to him, "but I can't stop to talk now. I really need to use the bathroom!" She couldn't help but think how she would never have given any of her suitors any information about her bladder habits when she was younger, but senior status had somehow made her more forthcoming and less inhibited. Or maybe conniving. In truth, although her bladder often did make her rush to get to the nearest bathroom, this was not one of those moments.

Hubert Darby stood totally befuddled, twisting his upper torso around to look at her as Essie stormed down the narrow hallway towards her room. He barely noticed as Opal and Marjorie whizzed by on either side of him with their walkers, led by Fay in her motor chair. Hubert just stood there, shaking his head and looking forlorn. Pulling a large white cloth hanky from his pants pocket, he wiped sweat from his forehead and headed back towards the lobby.

Essie continued on down her hallway, oblivious of the string of three women following her. She reached her doorway. She knew it was hers not because of its location or even the "B114" plastered on the door. She knew it was hers because the door was festooned with a jaunty Christmas elf. Essie–like most residents–always decorated her door for upcoming holidays. As Christmas was only days away, she had put her cute little elf on her door because he always made her feel in a Christmas-y mood. That, and because her late husband John had always adored the little fellow and had insisted that he reside on the front door of their home every Christmas–no matter where they had lived. When Essie saw her Christmas elf she grabbed her door handle and opened her door. Carefully, she wheeled her walker inside and turned around to close the door behind her.

"Oh, no you don't!" cried Opal, arriving at the doorway along with Marjorie and Fay and barring Essie from closing it with the left front wheel of her walker. "Just what are you up to, Essie Cobb?"

"Yes, Essie!" agreed Marjorie, pushing her walker through the door frame along with Opal, effectively preventing Essie from closing her own door. Fay remained in her wheelchair directly behind the two women.

"I have to go!" cried Essie, giving them her little fake bladder dance.

"Then go!" ordered Opal, "we'll just wait until you're done!" She barreled into Essie's small apartment, followed by Marjorie and finally Fay. The three women lined up like a firing squad in the middle of Essie's living room and Essie felt like a prisoner making her final request. She looked at her three friends and at her wide-open front door and then at the basket beneath her walker seat where the infant was hopefully still sleeping. Anyone could walk down the outside hallway at any moment, she thought. If a staff member walked by and the baby cried, I'd be in trouble. Worse, yet, the baby would be taken from me—and Maria might never see her child again!

Making a quick decision, Essie rolled her walker over to the door and quietly closed it. She gestured for the three women to take seats, which they did. Fay remained in her wheelchair by Essie's only outside window on the far side of her living room. A hanging row of Christmas lights decorated the top of her window. Through the blinds, Essie could see that a light snow had begun to fall.

"I thought you said you had to pee," said Marjorie.

"Marjorie," said Opal, aghast, "such language!"

"She said it!" replied Marjorie. Essie's living room smelled noticeably of Christmas because she had strategically placed several fragrance dispensers on tables around the room to elicit holiday memories whenever she entered her apartment.

"Quiet, you two!" interjected Essie, looking at her arguing friends now seated together on Essie's small sofa, their walkers parked in front of them. They looked like two petulant siblings being forced to sit next to each other for their annual Christmas photo. Essie rolled her walker over to her favorite lounge chair and sat. "I'm fine. I don't have to pee. I just had to get back to my room."

"You're here!" said Opal. "So what did Santos want with you in the kitchen? And why did you have to rush out of the dining room so fast that you couldn't even stop long enough to tell us about it?"

"Because," said Essie, "Santos asked me to do him a favor. And I . . . uh . . . promised to keep something for him."

"What, Essie?" asked Marjorie. Her green eyes sparkled merrily. Marjorie was always up for a caper.

"Why would one of the kitchen workers want you to keep something for him?" added Opal. Opal was more circumspect than Marjorie and would only become involved if the cause was just.

"Is it drugs?" suggested Marjorie with a salacious grin.

"Of course not, Marjorie!" replied Essie, "I guess he asked me because he had heard about everything I had done to help Bob Weiderley." She fingered the little winter snow globe that she kept on the end table next to her lounger. The swirling snowstorm inside helped to calm her.

"So?" continued Opal. "What did he give you to keep?" Fay motored closer. All three of Essie's friends glared at her with wide-open eyes.

"You all promise not to tell?" Essie asked, looking directly at each of them one at a time.

"It's not a bomb, is it?" shouted Marjorie suddenly, her delicate, little mouth forming a wide 'o'.

"No," replied Essie, "it's totally not a bomb—or drugs—or anything dangerous. Why would you even think such a thing, Marjorie?"

"So?" continued Opal, "What is it, Essie? Put up or shut up!" The women looked at Essie and then, before she could respond, an ear-splitting cry rocked the small room.

Chapter Four

"There are three reasons for breast-feeding: the milk is always at the right temperature; it comes in attractive containers; and the cat can't get it."
–Irena Chalmers

"Essie? What was that?" demanded Opal, her body frozen as her eyes darted around like one of those cat clocks with the bulging eyes. As another cry shot forth, the three women all turned their heads to the source of the loud noise--the seat of Essie's walker, which sat in front of their hostess, her knees now flush against the leather seat and her hands firmly gripping the rubber handle bars.

"I . . . uh . . ." stammered Essie, looking from one friend to another, leaning forward as if covering the source of the cry might make it disappear.

"What do you have in your walker basket?" asked Marjorie. Essie scowled and looked around. It was obvious that she couldn't hide her secret from her friends now. She'd been found out. She carefully lifted the leather seat and leaned it against the walker's handlebars. Then, reaching inside the basket, she gathered the makeshift blankets together and gently removed the tiny baby, now squirming and whining pitifully. She scooted closer to Opal and

Marjorie seated on the sofa to show them what she held.

"Oh, my God!" intoned Opal. "It's a baby!" Her hand went to her mouth.

"Essie, where did you get a baby?" squealed Marjorie, her eyes bulging. Both women scooted closer to Essie on the sofa and bent towards the child. Fay pushed the button on her wheelchair and moved even closer into the group. She stopped her wheelchair when her knees bumped into the back of Essie's walker. The foursome was now almost head to head, bending over the little tot.

"His face is cut!" noted Opal with a cry.

"Oh, Opal, look at his leg! See that bruise!" added Marjorie.

"Yes," said Essie, "that's part of the problem. The baby's father is evidently abusive . . . to the baby . . . and the mother."

"Where is the mother?" asked Opal.

"It's a long story," replied Essie, "but I promised Santos I'd guard this little one until Santos's friend Maria . . . the mother. . . returns . . . ."

"When will that be?" demanded Opal, her long thin fingers gesturing emphatically. "You can't keep a baby in your apartment, Essie. What if Violet finds out?"

"Oh, yes!" agreed Marjorie, "Violet will have your hide, Essie, if she finds out!" Marjorie said this with such vigor that baby Antonio let out another of his loud yelps. As Essie tried unsuccessfully to rock the baby, Fay quietly bent across Essie's walker handlebars and reached for the little bundle.

"Fay wants to hold him!" said Marjorie. "Then me next!" Essie passed the baby to Fay across the walker. Immediately, Fay tightened the baby's blankets and pulled the baby snuggly into her body. She placed her little finger in the baby's mouth and he began to suck vigorously.

"He's hungry!" exclaimed Opal, observing the child's reaction.

"Oh, no!" cried Essie. "Santos didn't give me any formula for him. I guess he thought Maria would be back by now to nurse him!"

"Fay seems to know what to do with him for now," noted Marjorie. "Look how she's wrapped him up really tight. I've read that that helps keep babies calm. Indians used to wrap their babies like that."

"Yes," said Opal, "and they held them tightly too; they called them a papoose."

"A sweet little papoose," agreed Essie. All three women smiled at Fay who appeared oblivious to everything except the tiny child who was now starting to calm in her arms.

"Essie," said Marjorie, "you're going to have to feed him, you know. You can't wait for this Maria woman to return. Who knows when she'll be back--if ever?"

"If ever? Why do you say that?" demanded Essie.

"Stop it, you two!" cried Opal, with a firm shake of her hands. "We can discuss the why's and where for's later. Right now, we have to figure out how to feed this child–and satisfy his obvious hunger before he cries again and notifies all of Happy Haven of his presence."

"How can we feed him, Opal?" asked Essie. "I don't have any formula–and I doubt there's anyone at Happy Haven who has any either. It's not like we have a lot of pregnant women or new mothers here."

"Then, we'll just have to make do with a substitute," said Opal, rising and pushing her walker around the little group and towards Essie's small kitchen area. She began opening cupboard doors. Essie always admired Opal's typically professional, take-charge attitude.

"What are you looking for, Opal?" asked Essie. "Tell me, and I'll tell you where it is if I have it."

"Do you have any plastic gloves?" asked Opal, her straight back to the group, as she continued to fling cupboard doors open and shut.

"You mean like mittens?" asked Essie.

"No, plastic gloves, like nurses use when they give you an injection," Opal replied over her shoulder.

"I don't think . . . . Wait! I do have a pair of rubber cleaning gloves under my bathroom sink, I think. Claudia brought them over once when she planned to clean my bathroom and just left them here. She never used them. They're still in the package."

"I'll get them, Opal," offered Marjorie, already on her feet and pushing her walker towards Essie's small bathroom.

"Fay," ordered Opal from the kitchen, "you just keep that child quiet while the three of us figure out what and how to feed him. That's the first order of business. Because if we don't feed him soon, we won't be able to keep him quiet much longer." She pulled out a can from the cupboard above Essie's sink. "How long have you had this can, Essie? Oh, never mind. The expiration date says . . . oh, it's okay. It's still good."

"What is it?" asked Essie, rising and heading her walker toward Opal. "I don't have any formula."

"No," agreed Opal, "but you do have Vigor, which has . . ." Opal squinted as she read the miniscule words on the side of the blue can. "Oh, how do they expect anyone to read this?" She gyrated her glasses around on her face in an attempt to make the small letters come into focus. "But it's 'full of protein' and it's 'easily digestible' according to the label. That's what we want for the baby, don't we?"

"I guess," said Essie. She grabbed the can from Opal and turned on the sink faucet, shaking the can and running it under the hot water. Finally, she opened a drawer next to her small sink and removed a punch-top can opener. With Opal holding the can steady on the counter, Essie used both hands to punch two holes in the top of the protein drink can. "It's been quite a while since I've had to open a can with one of these things! There's nothing like having arthritis in your fingers!"

"I found them!" exclaimed Marjorie, returning from the bathroom, and holding out a plastic container which showed a pair of yellow rubber gloves inside. Opal grabbed the box and ripped it open.

"I need scissors, Essie," said Opal, examining the length and width of the different fingers on one of the gloves. Essie scooted her walker back to her desk in the living room and extracted a small pair of shears from a container on the top of her desk. She quickly returned to the kitchen and handed them to Opal.

"Not sure how much to cut off," pondered Opal, as she held up one of the fingers of the glove and placed the scissors at the very tip.

"Maybe you should use a needle," suggested Marjorie, "most nipples on bottles have extremely small openings if I remember."

"Do you have a needle, Essie?" asked Opal.

"I have a sewing kit somewhere, I think," said Essie, rolling her walker towards the bedroom. At this point, the baby let out another cry and Fay increased her rocking speed and held him even tighter. She lowered her head to the baby's face and started making soft humming noises in his ear.

"Keep that little papoose quiet, Fay," called Opal from across the room.

"Fay does seem to have a way with babies," whispered Marjorie to Opal.

"She does," agreed Opal, "but even she can't make him not hungry just by rocking him."

Essie returned from her bedroom with a plastic box on the seat of her walker. She moved towards Opal and Marjorie and opened the small container and carefully lifted out a small apple-shaped pin cushion. From it, she pulled a long silver needle.

"I can do it," said Essie, as she placed the box on the ground and sat down on her walker, needle in hand. Opal handed her the rubber glove. Bringing glove and needle within an inch of her eyes, Essie stabbed the tiniest glove finger with the needle several times. "There! I think that will do! Try it out, Opal."

With that, Opal grabbed the glove and moved back to Essie's sink. She turned on the faucet and allowed the hot water to fill the rubber glove. Essie and Marjorie gathered around her and watched as a small stream of water squirted out of the end of the punctured glove finger. Opal ran more hot water through the glove, shaking it up and down in an attempt to sanitize it.

"That looks about right!" declared Essie. Opal held up the glove over the sink and held it open while Marjorie poured protein drink from the opened can into the glove. As the can had not been refrigerated, the liquid was a pleasant room temperature.

"Wait!" cried Essie, running back to her desk, "We need this!" She grabbed a large rubber band from a ring of many bands that surrounded a small can full of pencils. Bringing the rubber band to the kitchen, she wound it around the top of the glove while Marjorie kept her fingers pinched on the end of the glove finger where Essie had created a hole. Then the three women carefully brought the entire glove-drinking contraption over to the middle of the living room where Fay was seated still rocking the baby. They slipped the glove under Fay's hand and Fay grabbed onto the makeshift nipple and gently substituted it for her finger in the hungry baby's mouth. All four women remained breathless as they waited to see if baby Antonio would be able to drink from the glove-bottle they had just made and, more important, if he would accept Vigor, the adult protein drink as a substitute for baby formula. In a few seconds, the sounds of contented sucking replaced the pitiful cries of before.

"He seems to like it," noted Essie. They all smiled and ever so quietly returned to their seats while Fay continued to feed the infant.

"That was a close call, Essie," said Opal, "but if any staff member heard that baby cry, they're going to come checking on your room . . . and you're going to be in trouble."

"Yes, Essie," agreed Marjorie. "We're glad we could help you out in this emergency, but you can't keep this baby here. You have to figure out a different plan."

"What?" asked Essie. "If I let the staff know about Antonio, they'll report him to social services and put him in a foster home. Then Maria may never get him back."

"If she deserted him," offered Opal, "she shouldn't get him back!"

"She didn't desert him. You don't know the whole story, Opal!" argued Essie.

"Then tell us," Opal snapped back. But before Essie could open her mouth to explain, there was a knock on her door.

Chapter Five
"Diaper backward spells repaid. Think about it."
–Marshall McLuhan

The four women froze. No one said a word as they looked back and forth from one to the other. Then, Essie quickly motioned for Marjorie and Fay to go to her bedroom with the baby and for Opal to stay seated on the sofa. As the women hurried to their appointed positions, Essie moved to the door, all the while giving Opal a "shh"ing gesture.

"Lorena!" announced Essie loudly as she peeked through a crack in the doorway.

"You expectin' someone else, Miss Essie?" asked a large black woman almost bursting out of her turquoise trousers and matching print uniform top. In her thick curly locks she wore a small crocheted Santa face as a hair decoration. "You ready for your night pills and your pj's, Miss Essie, or you gonna' keep me coolin' my heels out here in the hall all night?" demanded the aide, hands on hips, with a rhythmical roll of her head and eyes.

"No, Lorena," said Essie, cringing, "I guess you can come in." She rolled back inside and the plump nurses' aide followed, shutting the door behind herself. "Oh, uh, Lorena, this is my friend Opal. She stopped by for a . . . a visit."

Lorena stopped in her tracks just inside the door as she observed the other woman sitting primly on the sofa. Both older ladies were smiling broad Cheshire cat grins as if they had just been caught with their hands in the proverbial cookie jar.

"Miss Opal," said Lorena, nodding in greeting. "It's nice to see Miss Essie making friends."

"Oh, Essie and I are tablemates," explained Opal calmly to the aide. "We've been friends for a long time. We were . . . uh . . . selecting a secret Santa gift!"

"Planning a surprise party!" said Essie at the same time.

"How nice!" replied Lorena, befuddled, as she went about her regular routine of opening Essie's kitchen cupboard and removing a locked pill box. "My husband thought he was gettin' me a surprise Christmas present last year, but the doofus went and hid it under our bed. Not too bright, huh? As if I don't look there just before Christmas. What about your pajamas, Essie?" She used a small key from around her wrist to unlock the box.

"Oh!" exclaimed Essie. "I forgot! I didn't realize it had gotten so late, Lorena! Opal and I must have lost track of time we were so busy . . . uh, planning that Christmas . . ."

"Surprise," supplied Opal, smiling expansively for Lorena. "We're planning a Christmas surprise party for one of our friends who has a birthday near Christmas and she never gets a party." Opal gave Essie a knowing nod to indicate that their stories now coincided.

"Who's that?" asked Lorena casually, turning back around to the women.

"Uh, it's . . ." Essie stammered.

"I don't think you'd know her," added Opal.

"Does she live at Happy Haven?" asked Lorena, arms crossed, staring pointedly down her large round nose at the women.

"Yes . . ." admitted Essie.

"Then I know her," said Lorena with a caustic grin.

"Of course," continued Essie, "but we really don't want to mention her name because it's–you know–a surprise!" Lorena glanced back and forth from the calculatingly charming faces of the two little old ladies sitting before her. It was clear from Lorena's face that she realized that they were up to something--what she didn't know--but it was probably more than just planning a surprise birthday party.

"Do you want me to come back later to get your pj's on, when you two is all done with your big party plans?" asked Lorena as she brought over the pill box and a glass of water. She handed Essie the glass and proceeded to drop pills into Essie's free palm from each of the compartments of the pill box.

"Oh, no!" cried Essie, between swallowing each of her bedtime pills. She finished the pills and handed the empty glass back to Lorena, who took it back to the kitchen and locked up the pill box and replaced it in the top cupboard.

"You shouldn't have to come back later, Lorena," added Opal, sitting up stiffly on the sofa and glancing surreptitiously at Essie's bedroom door. So far, there had been no baby sounds since the aide had entered Essie's apartment.

"I'll just get my pj's," said Essie, "and you can help me get dressed right now!"

Lorena started for the bedroom door where Essie was also headed.

"I can get your jams, Miss Essie!" she said, "You stay here and chat with your friend!"

"Oh, no, Lorena! I can do it!" exclaimed Essie, cutting the aide off with her walker and backing up into her bedroom and pulling the door closed behind her. Lorena stared at Essie's retreating form with a scowl and then turned back to Opal, still seated on the sofa.

"I don't think I ever know Miss Essie to have guests," she said pointedly to Opal.

"Isn't that funny," agreed Opal, endeavoring to engage the aide in conversation and distract her attention from Essie's bedroom door. "I hardly ever invite anyone to my apartment either. I guess it's because our rooms are so small, you know, and, of course, we all do talk among ourselves so much at every meal that I guess we just don't feel the need to chat any more outside of dinner times. You know how that is, I'm sure. And, of course, at night, we're all so busy getting ready for bed, what with our pills and getting our nightwear on and all the other things, that entertaining is just terribly far from our minds, that . . ."

Her ramblings were cut short when Essie suddenly returned from the bedroom, pulling the door shut behind her and dangling a pair of blue nylon pajamas over the handlebars of her walker. She rolled quickly over to Lorena, handed her the clothes, and sat down in her lounge chair.

"Should I go, Essie?" asked Opal.

"Maybe your friend should . . . you are getting ready for bed, Essie," suggested Lorena.

"No! Of course not!" pronounced Essie firmly. "We're all women! Just get on with it, Lorena! And hurry up! Opal, you stay! There's no reason for you to leave!" Lorena, following orders, quickly helped Essie remove her shoes and socks, trousers, shirt, and underwear, and even more quickly slip into her pj's. Opal sat turned away on the sofa politely, fidgeting, and glancing every so often at Essie's bedroom door.

"My goodness, Miss Essie," remarked Lorena, as she dressed the older woman. "I've never seen you so anxious to get ready for bed in my entire time at Happy Haven!"

"There!" exclaimed Essie when she was finally outfitted in her nighttime attire. "Thank you so much, Lorena! I'm all set now!"

"You are indeed, Miss Essie," agreed Lorena, rising from the floor. She stood towering over the two old ladies seated before her, hands on her ample hips. "You know, if I didn't know any better, Miss Essie, I'd say that you were up to something . . ."

"Up to something?" asked Essie, looking up into Lorena's gleaming face. "What do you mean, Lorena?"

"About this surprise party you're planning?"

"Yes?" repeated Opal.

"You know," suggested Lorena, glancing back and forth from Essie to Opal in an apparent attempt to see if either would reveal their intentions, "this plan you have for one of your friends? It wouldn't happen to be Bob Weiderley, would it?"

"What?!" exclaimed Essie. "Oh, I see what you mean, Lorena! You think Opal and I are plotting this party for Bob . . . ."

"I wouldn't put it past you, Miss Essie," interrupted Lorena, grabbing her clipboard from the sink counter and marking on it with a pencil from her front pocket. "I mean, everyone knows about what you did for Mr. Weiderley! You are somewhat of a celebrity around here!"

"That's ridiculous!" said Essie, with a modest huff. "I just did what anyone would do to help a friend . . . and Opal and I are just two friends who happen to be sitting here in my living room together planning a friendly little celebration for a friend."

"That's it," agreed Opal, nodding authoritatively. "Just a friendly little celebration!"

"Then, you two ladies enjoy your planning," said Lorena with a final shrug. She zipped over to Essie's kitchen counter. "Essie, what's this empty can of Vigor doing here? Are you drinking this stuff as a bedtime snack? I mean, if you want I can bring you something tastier than this junk."

"That's mine!" said Opal, jumping into the conversation at about the same time that Essie said, "I just wanted to try it!"

"Whichever one of you drank it," said Lorena with a chuckle, "doesn't matter. You ladies can drink whatever dreck you like; I just want you to know that I can bring you something better. How about some milkshakes?" She tossed the empty can in the wastebasket under Essie's kitchen sink.

"No! No!" argued Essie, "I really like . . . we really like Vigor! Pitiful Pete, Lorena! Don't tell on us! We just like the 'dreck'! Sorry!"

"Nothing to be sorry about, Miss Essie, and I'm sure not gonna' tell on you," said Lorena, with a shrug. "Okay, you two, I'm out of here! Enjoy your visit!" The nurses's aide closed up the cupboard and slipped out quietly through Essie's door.

Immediately upon Lorena's departure, Essie rose, grabbed her walker, and wheeled it into her bedroom. Opal followed quickly on her heels. Inside Essie's small bedroom, they found Fay and Marjorie sitting knees to knees–Fay still in her wheelchair and Marjorie on the edge of Essie's bed. Baby Antonio was at present in Marjorie's arm's chugging away at the Vigor-filled rubber glove. The glove was now almost totally depleted of its contents.

"She's gone!" announced Essie to the two women. Opal stuck her head through the small bedroom doorway. There was barely enough room for two seated and one standing. Opal was forced to remain in the doorway.

"That was a really close call, Essie," scolded Opal from behind. "I think she suspects us!"

"Of course she suspects us," agreed Essie. "Didn't you hear her? She thinks we're planning some extravagant shindig for Bob, I guess. So . . . that's just what we'll let her think."

"This is all one big lie, Essie," continued Opal, "I hate lying! I'm afraid this will come back to haunt us . . . or, should I say, haunt you!"

"Shoots and boots!" responded Essie to the voice behind her, "I'm not afraid of Lorena. Right now, all I'm concerned about is this little fellow! How's he doing Marjorie?"

"He drank most all of the Vigor," whispered Marjorie, continuing to rock the baby. Fay was totally focused on the little infant's face.

"I hope you're not killing that child with that stuff," added Opal, "You heard what Lorena said about it, Essie! She called it dreck!"

"He seems just fine," said Marjorie. "I think we did the right thing! I see you're in your pj's, Essie."

"Yes, and hopefully, that means that no one else will come knocking on my door!"

"Until morning," said Opal, deflating the group mood. "What are you going to do when your morning aide arrives, Essie?"

"I guess I'll figure that out tomorrow. Isn't that what Scarlett O'Hara said? Tomorrow is another day!" replied Essie. "Maybe Santos will have found Maria by then."

"Oh my God!" said Marjorie with disgust.

"What's wrong?" asked Essie.

" Mother Nature!" said Marjorie, "Antonio just pooped his pants! Guess that Vigor went right through him."

"Eww!" added Opal from the doorway, holding her nose. "That smells disgusting!"

As the new odor began to waft around the small room, Fay quickly turned her wheelchair around and headed into Essie's small bathroom.

"Now, where has she gone?" asked Marjorie.

"To get away from the smell," suggested Opal.

"I hope she doesn't expect to find diapers in there!" added Essie.

"If you have them, Fay will find them!" said Opal, as Fay returned holding a pink cardboard box on her lap.

"That's not diapers, Fay!" cried Essie. Fay held up a box labeled Reliables. "Where'd you find that? That's a box of those adult incontinence pads my daughter Claudia bought me ages ago, hoping I'd try them. I refuse to wear those stupid things. I'd rather make a mad dash to the restroom than to run around all day with wet pants."

Fay quickly opened the box and extracted one of the thick pads. Expertly tearing and reshaping the item, she reassembled it until it was designed to perfectly fit a little baby boy's bottom (and front). As the other three women saw what Fay was doing, Essie zipped back to her desk in the living room and returned with scissors and sticky tape. Marjorie gently removed the disposable paper diaper presently on the baby and handed it to Opal who disposed of it in Essie's kitchen waste basket. Then, Fay slipped the clean homemade diaper on baby Antonio who cooed quietly throughout the entire procedure. Marjorie then handed Antonio to Fay who rocked him gently in her arms.

"You have enough of these Reliables in this box, Essie, to last Antonio for a few days," noted Opal.

"Hopefully, he won't need them," said Essie, "Hopefully, Santos will find Antonio's mother soon and our babysitting days will be over."

"Hopefully," agreed Opal.

"Hopefully," repeated Marjorie.

Fay just smiled at little Antonio, the two of them seemingly lost in a spell.

"What about that cut on his face?" asked Marjorie.

"And the bruise on his leg?" added Opal.

"I've got disinfectant for the cut," suggested Essie as she whizzed back to her bathroom and returned with a tube of cream. Opal quickly swabbed a small amount on the baby's facial cut.

"Ladies!" said Essie. "This baby is our responsibility now." The four women looked at the baby and then at each other. Their group smile quickly turned into a look of worry.

Chapter Six
"People who say they sleep like a baby usually don't have one."
–Leo J. Burke

Hours later after her three friends had–somewhat reluctantly–left her room and their opportunity to cuddle and coo over baby Antonio, Essie now found herself alone with the infant. It was unlikely, she reasoned, that anyone else would come knocking on her door at this time of night. The hands on her golden perpetual clock that Pru's oldest child Arthur had given her, pointed to exactly midnight. The last time Essie remembered seeing the hands of a clock register midnight had occurred the previous evening when she was making one of her many middle of the night bathroom runs.

"I guess we're a lot alike," she whispered to baby Antonio, lying beside her on her bed. When she spoke, Antonio shook his tiny fists gleefully and gyrated his pudgy legs back and forth as if he were riding an imaginary bicycle. "Only you don't have to make bathroom runs when you need to go!" He made a sweet gurgling noise and appeared to look right at Essie.

"I know you don't know me," she said to him, "but you are a cheerful little guy!" She smiled over at him and tweaked his cheek. Antonio giggled and pedaled his feet faster. Essie looked him over from top to bottom. He appeared to be full-term and healthy--at least if size and weight were any indication. She guessed him to be about eight or nine pounds--a good chunk for a newborn. He sported a full head of black hair which looked beautiful against his lovely tan skin. His cheeks were round and the right one had a dimple directly below the gash. Every time he smiled, it dipped in. Essie was enjoying trying to make him smile just so she could see the dimple.

"Doesn't look like you plan on doing any sleeping, little guy," she said with a sigh. She looked around her small bedroom. It wouldn't be safe to let the baby stay in bed with her. She'd heard horrible tales about some mothers doing just that and suffocating infants when they rolled over on them in their sleep. "Guess I'd better transfer you back to your walker basket before either one of us drifts off."

Essie scooted to the edge of her bed and dropped her feet down until she found her bedroom slippers. Then, standing carefully with the help of her walker which was beside the edge of the bed, she stood up. Turning back to the baby, she reached out for him and pulled him closer to her. As she slid him along the sheets, baby Antonio started fussing and by the time Essie had him on the bed's edge, he'd started to howl.

"Oh, no!" she said out loud. "I thought this was going too well." She looked at the alarm clock on her end table. It was well past midnight now. The child was probably hungry. Anticipating that this would happen, Opal and Marjorie had prepared an extra rubber gloveful of Vigor and left it on Essie's kitchen counter. "Wait here, Antonio," she whispered to the baby as she scooted the infant further towards the center of the bed for safe keeping. Then, grabbing her walker, she headed toward her kitchen, grabbed the filled glove and zipped back to the bedroom before Antonio had emitted a second cry. Essie parked her walker and sat on the bed next to him, leaning against the headboard. She removed the rubber band that Marjorie had tied around the finger with the needle opening and, picking up Antonio in her arms, gently slid the rubber appendage into his awaiting mouth. The little boy latched onto the finger immediately and started sucking furiously.

"Holy coyote!" exclaimed Essie to the little boy in her arms, "you are one hungry fellow!" Almost instantly, Antonio's violent feet and arm movements slowed and he calmed as he drank the make-shift formula. "Sorry I can't provide real mother's milk, Antonio, but I'm all dried up in that area!" She chuckled to herself and Antonio seemed to respond to her joke and giggled back at her while he drank.

When the infant finished the formula, had a new Reliables diaper on, and was sleeping soundly again, Essie gently transferred him to the basket in her walker and covered him with several soft towels from her bathroom. Then she wheeled him with her as she moved to her kitchen and prepared another serving of Vigor for when he next became hungry. She took the spare formula-filled glove back to the bedroom and placed it and several spare fake diapers on her end table so she could get to them if she needed them in the middle of the night. Then, as Antonio appeared to be sleeping soundly in the walker basket, Essie crawled into her bed and fell almost immediately to sleep.

Normally, Essie never slept deeply. Because of her weak bladder, she frequently awakened several times at night to go to the bathroom. Tonight was no different. When she felt the urge to pee, Essie roused herself and started to climb out of bed. Abruptly, she remembered the infant in her walker next to her bed. Cautiously, she glanced at Antonio who was sleeping peacefully. Essie glanced at her clock. It was now after two in the morning. She made her way into her bathroom holding onto the wall because she didn't want to chance disturbing the sleeping child by moving the walker. When she returned and was climbing back into bed, she realized that her biggest challenge was looming and that she probably shouldn't avoid considering it until morning. That was, what to do with Antonio when her morning aide, DeeDee, arrived at seven to get her dressed and give her her morning medications. Hmmm. DeeDee always came directly into her bedroom. She just knocked to announce her presence, but then she walked right in.

A plan began to hatch in Essie's mind. DeeDee typically didn't go into Essie's bathroom unless Essie asked her to. It would be close, but if Antonio would cooperate by being quiet during the few minutes that

DeeDee would be in her apartment, maybe Essie could manage to maintain her secret for a while longer. She lay down on her bed and dozed for a few more hours, but at six she decided that she'd better get busy if she was going to pull off operation "secret baby."

As Essie started to slide out of bed and move around her small bedroom, holding on to furniture and walls for support, she could hear her charge stirring in the walker. Little cooing sounds began to emanate from the basket. She realized that she'd probably have to feed Antonio first before she could do much else. Sitting on her bed, and grabbing the glove device from her end table where she had left it, she scooped up Antonio in her arms and quickly began to feed him. The baby was hungry and quickly made short work of the entire contents of the glove. Afterwards, Essie changed the diaper that she now expected to be soiled. One thing for sure, this was a consistent little fellow. She hoped she could rely on his consistency for just another hour or so, until DeeDee was gone, and perhaps Santos had found his mother.

After changing the baby's makeshift diapers and placing him back in the walker basket, Essie quickly maneuvered the walker to her bathroom. She pulled out every towel she had from her cupboards and arranged them softly in the bottom of her bathtub and deposited the infant in the middle of her bathtub. Then, she gently closed the bathroom door, returned to her bedroom and opened her drawers and brought out a clean outfit to wear--a flowered blue shirt, navy pull-on trousers, white gym socks, clean panties and bra. She laid these items on the end of her bed and placed her tennis shoes on the floor beside them. As she looked at her clock again, the hands were just a few minutes before seven. DeeDee was often early. Essie could never really figure out why some days her aide was early and some days she was late, but Essie could pretty much count on DeeDee arriving within ten minutes one way or another of seven o'clock.

Today DeeDee was early. There was the typical knock on her front door and then Essie heard DeeDee Pritoni's cheerful voice, "Miss Essie! Time to get up!" DeeDee's face appeared in the bedroom doorway. A look of amazement replaced her casual expression. DeeDee's beautifully curved eyebrows rose alarmingly and her black ponytail bobbed.

"Miss Essie! You're up!" said DeeDee as she entered Essie's bedroom. "And you have clothes set out! Are these what you want to wear?"

"DeeDee," replied Essie, quickly and quietly, "I just couldn't sleep, so I decided to get up. I picked out what I want to wear so you can just help me slip these clothes on and give me my pills and I can get going. Okay?"

"Of course, Miss Essie!" agreed the young woman, moving into the room and expertly helping Essie dress for her day. This was a routine that the duo had accomplished together many times and each knew exactly when to stick out an arm or pull up or down. Soon, Essie was dressed and DeeDee headed to the living room and removed the pill box in the kitchen just as Lorena had done the previous evening. Essie followed her, carefully closing the bedroom door behind her.

"You surprise me, Miss Essie!" said DeeDee as she handed Essie a glass of water and a handful of five or six pills. "You're usually such a sleepyhead! Just what made you want to get up and get going so early today?" DeeDee tapped her toe as she eyed Essie slurping down her pills as if she were drinking a tasty daiquiri.

"Gumgle," mumbled Essie, continuing to swallow pills.

"No scowl?" questioned DeeDee, as she took back the glass Essie handed her. "You usually hate taking your pills."

"No,!" argued Essie, "I'm just anxious to get going."

"I know," said DeeDee, conspiratorially, "I bet it's Hubert Darby, isn't it? I think I heard someone say that he's sweet on you. Maybe you two have a rendezvous planned?" DeeDee's perfectly manicured eyebrows gyrated up and down lasciviously.

"I have no such thing!" exclaimed Essie. "And you can stop your Groucho Marx eyebrow routine, DeeDee! I'm an old lady and the only man I ever rendezvoused was my husband!"

DeeDee laughed as she put away the pills and glass.

"Okay, Miss Essie," she sang out as she opened Essie's front door, "if you say so! But that Hubert is one snazzy dresser, if you ask me!" Still chuckling, DeeDee closed the door and headed down the hallway.

"Hubert Darby, my foot," mumbled Essie, just as a cry sounded from her bathroom.

Chapter Seven

"It takes a village to raise a child."
–Author Unknown

Essie quickly rushed to her bathroom and moved to the bathtub where baby Antonio was screaming loudly. She hoped the walls of the small room would act as insulation of the sound or that her neighbor Clara was already at breakfast and couldn't hear the very loud noise. Clara was a busybody and would definitely complain to her or–worse–to the staff if she thought that Essie had a baby in her apartment. Essie bent over and lifted the infant from the tub. Her arthritis in her back ached as she tried to stand carrying the added weight. She placed Antonio over her shoulder and gently patted his back as she softly bounced him up and down. Almost immediately a loud burp emitted from the baby's mouth and he quieted noticeably. Essie placed him in the walker basket and wheeled him back into her bedroom. She sat on the edge of her bed and pondered what to do next.

She needed to go to breakfast, if for no other reason than to find Santos and discover what he'd found out about Antonio's mother. Had Maria returned? Did he know where she was? Essie knew she couldn't continue to keep the infant in her room for long. Should she take the baby with her and head to the dining hall? Or should she remain here and hope that Santos or one of her friends would come to her and let her know what was happening? Essie was exhausted. She had gotten even less sleep than she usually did. Worry over the baby had kept her up most of the night.

"Let's go!" she said finally to her little charge and she rose from her bed and gently tucked his arms into the basket and then cautiously lowered the lid. Moving with determination, she headed for her front door. As she opened the door and started to move her walker into the hallway, she was confronted by Opal, Marjorie, and Fay who motioned for her to return inside.

"Good morning, Essie," announced Opal, as the three women entered the apartment. Marjorie closed the door behind them. "We're here to cover for you."

"We're your back-up," added Marjorie. Fay had already lifted the seat on Essie's walker and had removed Antonio and was cradling him in her arms. She pressed her wheelchair's automatic button and her device whizzed her over to the window. Fay held Antonio up to the sparkling morning sunlight streaming into Essie's front window. The little boy giggled and cooed and tried to grab Fay's chin. Fay smiled and rubbed her face in the baby's tummy and they both laughed.

"Go to breakfast, Essie," ordered Opal, as she and Marjorie began moving around Essie's apartment. Opal headed to the kitchen and began preparing a new glove of formula. "I brought some reinforcements!" she announced as she opened the basket on her walker and removed several cans. "It's not Vigor, only a generic, but it should do. My son tried to get me to drink this horrible gunk too. These cans have been sitting above my sink for years. I think they're still good."

"That stuff could withstand a nuclear bomb!" called out Marjorie from the bathroom as she entered back into Essie's living room. "Essie, I've stacked up several more boxes of Reliables on your sink. I had some myself." Marjorie moved over and sat next to Fay and began gushing over the baby. "Oh, Fay, look, his little t-shirt is getting dirty! He needs something to wear besides just paper diapers and this old thing."

"Nell's bells, Marjorie!" cried Essie. "Outfitting this child is the least of our worries! Let's save infant fashion for another day and concentrate on the problem at hand!"

"Yes, let's!" agreed Opal still working efficiently at Essie's kitchen sink. "And the first problem is for you, Essie, to go to breakfast! We've all three eaten and we'll watch Antonio!"

"And besides, Santos told us he needs to speak to you!" added Marjorie.

"Why didn't you tell me that first?" demanded Essie. "Did he find Maria? What did he say about Antonio?"

"Essie," said Opal calmly. "He didn't say anything to us. He doesn't know that we know anything about the baby, remember? He merely asked us where you were. He just said he really needs to talk to you. We told him we would check on you and have you go straight to breakfast when we did. So, go!"

"Yes, go, Essie!" added Marjorie, extending a pointed finger towards the door. Opal gave Essie a "scoot" gesture and Fay smiled sweetly. Essie gave a sigh, turned tail, and headed out of her apartment.

She hated to leave the baby alone. Not that she didn't trust her three friends, but she felt uncomfortable leaving anyone in her place with the baby. Anything could happen. If the baby started crying and her friends couldn't calm him, she would be in trouble with the Happy Haven administration. She might even be evicted. Possibly. She wasn't sure. Violet didn't like her as it was. She was suspicious of Essie and watched her every movement. Even so, Essie was hungry and she needed to eat. She rolled her walker–now baby-free–into the dining hall and sat alone at her regular table.

Within a few seconds, Santos appeared beside her.

"Miss Essie," he said in a relieved voice. "I am so happy to see you. When you are not here for breakfast with other ladies, I am very worried." He bent over and whispered in Essie's ear. "Is baby okay, Miss Essie?"

Essie turned and patted Santos on the arm. She could see the worry in his eyes. "He's fine, Santos.

Opal, Marjorie, and Fay are taking good care of him now."

"You tell other ladies about Antonio, Miss Essie?" he asked, his face wrinkling in despair.

"Don't worry, Santos," replied Essie. "They are good people. They love babies. I told them about Maria and they will protect her secret–just like I will." She smiled gently again at the young man who appeared petrified that the child's existence might become public knowledge.

"I hope this is so, Miss Essie," said Santos. "Miss Marjorie and Miss Opal and Miss Fay are very nice ladies. You sure they not tell Miss Violet? I am very scared Miss Violet find out and take baby Antonio from Maria."

"We're trying very hard not to let anyone else find out about the baby, Santos," she replied in a whisper, patting his sleeve. "But, Santos, more important. What about Maria? Have you heard from her?"

Santos sighed deeply and stood up. He rubbed his hands over his face in a gesture of despair. "No, Miss Essie," he cried softly. "I hear nothing from Maria. I do not know where Maria is. I am very worried."

"This is not good," said Essie, shaking her head. "You know this woman, Santos. Do you think she has abandoned her baby? I mean, maybe all of this was just too much for her. Maybe she was so frightened of her husband and it was simply too hard to hide from him with a newborn infant. Maybe she's counting on you to protect the baby while she hides from her abusive mate."

"I do not think so, Miss Essie," continued Santos, speaking quietly as he pretended to collect dishes from the table. "Maria, she loves the baby! She does not come back for baby–this is very bad sign! I am afraid something bad happened to Maria."

"You mean, you think Gerald, her husband caught up with her and forced her to return to him?" asked Essie. "Do you think Gerald would seriously hurt Maria if she tried to leave him?"

"Si, I do, Miss Essie," replied Santos, stopping in his dish collecting and clutching a pile of dirty plates to his chest. His face was a portrait of pain.

"There must be some way to find out," said Essie. "The four of us–the four of us who sit at this table–we will try to take care of Antonio as long as we can, Santos, but this facility is not designed for infants, and eventually someone will discover that we have a newborn child in my apartment. And once that happens, I won't be able to keep the baby's presence a secret."

"Miss Essie," said Santos, his eyes sad and drooping, "please just watch Antonio a little bit longer. I will try to find Maria." He stood taller, his chin lifted.

"Tell me what you plan to do, Santos," said Essie. "Is there anything we can do to help track her down? Maybe call some of her relatives or friends?"

"I cannot do that, Miss Essie," said Santos, "I do not know Maria's friends or relatives. They are all in Mexico. I am very sorry."

"Santos," said Essie after contemplating this information, grabbing his shirt as the young man turned to the kitchen. "What is Maria's last name?"

"Compton," he said. "Maria Valdez Compton. She marry that Gerald Compton, the cabrón!" He ground his teeth and clenched his fists.

"And Gerald Compton works here in Reardon?" asked Essie, ignoring the young waiter's epithet.

"Si, Miss Essie," replied Santos, "Gerald build the houses. I not know where, but I remember Maria say it. It sound like flowers."

"Flowers?" she asked.

"Si, Miss Essie," he said with a shrug, "Like orchidea or—how you say—asafrán? I not very good at flowers."

"It's something," said Essie, nodding. "Now, can I have some eggs and bacon before I begin my detecting, Santos? And, please, don't let them burn the bacon!"

Santos smiled tentatively and headed off into the kitchen with his pile of dishes.

Chapter Eight

"I don't particularly like babies. I don't mind them for about four minutes. That's my max. After that I can't quite see what everyone's fussing about."
–Hugh Grant

Essie made short work of her breakfast. Her speed was partially because she was anxious to return to her apartment and tend to the baby. It was also partially because she didn't have anyone to talk to. Essie enjoyed her meals primarily because she enjoyed chatting with her tablemates and sipping her coffee. Without this camaraderie, all she could do was look around the dining hall at the few stragglers like herself who were lingering over their coffee too.

An announcement boomed out over the Happy Haven public address system.

"Residents," said the friendly young female voice, "don't forget today is book day. Anyone who wishes to take the bus to the library, be at the front door by ten this morning. Also, don't forget that we will have carolers from the Logan Street elementary school coming to sing to us this afternoon at four in the family room. Everyone will want to come down and listen to the beautiful Christmas music." Normally, Essie would be one of the first residents at such a program, but she doubted that she'd be able to attend today if she still had charge of baby Antonio. She couldn't very well take him to a vocal music program in the family room. As she mused about her activities, she felt a tap on her shoulder. She turned and looked up into the adoring eyes of Hubert Darby. Hubert was dressed this morning in a festive green corduroy jacket. A sprig of holly was attached to his lapel. In his hands, he held a gift box wrapped in red and gold tinfoil paper.

"Miss Essie," announced Hubert, thrusting the gift towards her. "This is for you." Essie was flustered as she accepted the gift. She was not used to receiving gifts from other residents—particularly male residents. Most residents didn't have any means to purchase presents for their friends, unless they had a relative buy them. For that reason, most did not exchange gifts. When birthdays occurred, residents typically gathered for a celebration in the dining hall and Happy Haven provided a cake and candles and everyone sang "Happy Birthday!" That was generally enough present for most residents. It was certainly enough for Essie. The last thing she needed was more stuff cluttering up her apartment.

"It's . . .uh . . . peanut brittle, Miss Essie," continued Hubert. He smiled a cheesy grin but his eyes were unable to focus on her face.

"Hubert," Essie replied tentatively, "I can't eat peanut brittle much anymore because it's so . . . hard to chew."

Hubert's face sank. "I'm sorry, Miss Essie," he stammered. "I thought you would like it. I didn't think

... about...." His voice trailed away. He scowled and his entire large forehead wrinkled. He appeared to be contemplating a serious problem, not the properties of candy.

"But, I'm very honored that you thought to buy this for me, Hubert," said Essie, jumping in. This was the most voluble she had ever heard Hubert Darby and she didn't want to discourage his efforts at communication—nor his sweet gesture. "I will enjoy it ... even if I have to just suck on a piece of it from time to time." She clutched the gift box to her chest and beamed up at Hubert.

Hubert's face turned a brilliant shade of red and he rocked back and forth on his tennis shoes just as he had done when he accosted her in her hallway the day before. Then, apparently lost for further words, he turned abruptly and shuffled out of the dining hall.

Essie smiled to herself and took another sip of her coffee as she contemplated her present predicament—and that even included Hubert Darby. She knew that she would probably have to take action to discover the whereabouts of Maria Valdez Compton, because it was obvious that Santos did not have the time or the language skills or the knowledge of the community to track the missing mother down on his own. Essie was going to have to get involved in finding this Maria—and she was going to have to keep her efforts quiet. Where to start? She now knew the woman's name, the husband's name, and a possible clue as to where the husband worked. She had immediately honed in on the fact that Maria's husband, Gerald Compton, worked for a company that had something to do with flowers. She would start there with a trip to her telephone directory.

As she was planning her next steps, she looked up and noticed a woman heading towards her table. She immediately recognized the woman as Clara Monroe, her next door neighbor. Oh dear, thought Essie. I hope she hasn't heard Antonio crying.

"Essie Cobb," said Clara, stopping on the other side of Essie's table and slamming her purse down in front of her. "Whatever is going on in your room?" Clara, wearing a severe high-necked black dress, with her long grey hair wrapped in a tight bun, looked for all the world like the stereotypical gossip that Essie perceived her neighbor to be.

Essie froze. Had the baby's cries been that noticeable? Yes, he had cried a few times, but each time he did, either she or one of her friends had immediately diverted his attention with food or rocking or something.

"What do you mean, Clara?" she asked cautiously, almost fearful that the determined little hen of a woman might pop her with the oversized black pocketbook that she was holding on to like some sort of weapon.

"It sounds like you're having some sort of convention over there in your apartment!" complained Clara, banging her purse on the table as she spoke in punctuation. "You must have had a crowd of fifty people there last night until all hours of the morning!" Clara clucked and harrumphed and added, "And with your television set playing so loud too!"

"Oh, Clara," interjected Essie, amused at Clara's exaggerations. "I guarantee I didn't have fifty people . . . or television."

Clara ignored Essie and continued, "And children! Lots of children, crying and whining!" This complaint, Essie noted was right on the mark. Clara continued listing Essie's bad deeds. "Did your relatives come in from out of town? My Lord, they are a noisy bunch, Essie!"

"No relatives, Clara," said Essie, sweetly and truthfully. "I promise you. Actually. . . just a few friends. Opal and Marjorie, my tablemates. You know them. And Fay–and she doesn't talk."

"Humph!" snorted the diminutive Clara, "Not likely! I've never heard so much noise! You have the loudest television set, Essie! I'm sure everyone in our hallway could hear it!"

"Really, Clara?" asked Essie, actually amused. "No one else from our hall has mentioned it. In fact, Clara, if it bothered you so much last night, why didn't you just knock on my door and complain about it then?"

"What?" cried Clara with a start, dropping her purse on the table. She pulled on the collar of her dress and fidgeted with the goiter on her neck. "I would never think of complaining, Essie. It's not in my nature!" She rose to her full height–which wasn't much–and, grabbing her purse in an apparent defensive move, walked purposefully out of the dining hall.

"Hmm," said Essie as she took another sip of coffee. She glanced down at her watch. Only twenty minutes had elapsed since she'd left her room. Surely, Opal, Marjorie, and Fay were handling baby Antonio just fine. Part of her felt a need to return to her apartment and check on his welfare. Another part of her felt the need to force herself to just sit at her table–tablemates or not–and relax for a moment. After all, they said that breakfast was the most important meal of the day. And she intended to at least let her food digest before returning into the excitement.

Essie glanced around. Even fewer residents remained over their coffee. Kitchen staff members were now busy cleaning up the room and preparing for the noon time meal. She could see many of them through the kitchen entrance working diligently chopping vegetables and preparing casseroles. She couldn't see Santos but was sure he was busy with his job and didn't have time to do the kind of detecting work that needed to be done to help Maria and her baby.

Over in the far corner by the window, two women were still eating. Essie didn't know who they were, but she thought that they were very slow. It was one thing to linger over a cup of coffee, but it was strange for them to still be actually eating. One lady was quietly nibbling on a piece of buttered toast and the other was bent over her plate, slurping small pieces of fried egg into her mouth. With each bite, her movements seemed to become slower and slower. Essie became intrigued with the egg-eating woman and the incredibly slow speed at which she consumed her meal. She wondered if this woman spent this amount of time eating her breakfast every day. Did her friend stay at the table merely to keep her company and did she attempt to match her eating speed to that of her friend? It was a puzzle, but one that Essie contemplated with only a casual interest.

However, Essie's interest in the slow eater increased when the woman suddenly looked up, bent over the side of her chair and vomited quite violently all over the floor. The woman's friend shrieked in alarm, standing up. Quickly, several kitchen workers descended on the two women to see what had happened. As they saw the situation, one stayed with the sick woman, who was still bent over, continuing to heave. The second ran swiftly out of the dining room. Within a few seconds, she returned, followed by a nurse who attended to the bent over woman. Shortly, the nurse helped the sick woman up and guided her past Essie, out of the dining hall. The second woman followed behind them. The two kitchen workers quickly cleaned up the mess and began to scrub the carpet with disinfectant.

In the years that Essie had been at Happy Haven, she'd seen many residents require medical attention. She had seen some faint. She had seen some fall and suffer injuries. She had even seen one resident die in front of her. This was the first time Essie had seen someone vomit. She wondered if the woman had experienced food poisoning or if she just had the flu. Either way, it wasn't good. Happy Haven was not filled with young Olympic athletes, so injuries, food poisoning, and harmful bacteria and viruses were not welcome here. On any other day, Essie might have been very curious about just what had happened to cause the slow eating lady to get sick so suddenly, but today was not one of those days. Today she had another, bigger problem.

Santos popped back into the dining hall, bringing coffee to a straggler near the entrance. As he whizzed past her, she grabbed his elbow.

"Santos," she said, looking up into his pre-occupied face, "if you hear anything about you-know-whom, please come by my apartment and let me know. I'm in B114."

"Si, Miss Essie," he replied, barely stopping on his way, "B114. I come see you if I hear anything." He expertly lifted the full cup of coffee in the air so it would not drip on Essie and then continued on his way towards the gentleman by the door. Essie grabbed her gift-wrapped box of peanut brittle–the token of affection from Hubert Darby–and headed back to her apartment.

Chapter Nine

"Father asked us, 'What was God's noblest work?' Anna said, 'Men,' but I said 'Babies.' Men are often bad, but babies never are."
–Louisa May Alcott

Back in her apartment, Essie found her three friends gathered around Fay's wheelchair which was parked in front of Essie's large front window. Fay was holding up baby Antonio as Marjorie reached up to the row of Christmas bells that hung from Essie's windows. As Marjorie touched each colorful bell and made it sound, the baby boy's eyes seemed to follow her hands. He cooed and gurgled in apparent delight.

"Essie, you're back!" cried Opal. "What's that present?"

"Oh, this," mumbled Essie as she placed the gift-wrapped box on her end table next to her snow globe, "just something from . . . Hubert."

"Hubert!" cried Marjorie. "He gave you a Christmas present, Essie?"

"It's just candy, Marjorie," replied Essie, "not the Hope Diamond." She sneered at her friend. "How's the baby?"

"Antonio loves music, Essie!" called out Marjorie from the window. "Watch!" She again punched the plastic bells in a row and, for certain, the baby did appear to wiggle and giggle in a full body response to the sound.

"He likes music," reiterated Opal. "He's probably going to be a musician." The three women left the window and moved into the center of Essie's living room. Essie sat down in her lounge chair, and Marjorie and Opal took their accustomed places on her sofa with Fay guiding her wheelchair to the center of the room—baby Antonio in her arms.

"So, Essie," began Marjorie, "did Santos find Antonio's mother?"

"No," replied Essie forlornly. She looked from one sad face to another and then all four women gazed at the little boy who apparently was now an orphan.

"I don't understand," continued Opal. "This woman just up and left her newborn child! How could a woman do such a thing? She doesn't deserve to keep him!"

"Now, don't say that, Opal," cautioned Essie. "According to Santos, Maria is protecting the baby. The father is abusive, remember?"

"So, where is she?" asked Opal. "I can understand wanting to take him away from the father, but why did she abandon him?"

"Santos says she's trying to protect him," said Essie, defensively.

"It doesn't look like it to me," argued Opal.

"I don't know, Opal," interjected Marjorie. "We don't know what that poor woman has gone through. The husband beat her. And don't forget he beat that poor helpless baby too! I think we should give her the benefit of the doubt! I think we should give her a little bit more time to try to work things out . . . whatever that entails."

"Yes," agreed Essie, "particularly if informing social services about Antonio might result in his being returned to the father. Surely we all agree that we can't let that happen."

"You really think the authorities would return the baby to the father?" asked Marjorie with incredulity.

"I wouldn't put it past them," said Essie. "He is the legal parent. The mother has abandoned the child so technically the father would get custody."

"We can't let that happen," said Opal, a fierce look of determination on her regal face.

"We can't," agreed Marjorie.

"Fay?" asked Essie. All three women looked at their quiet fourth member holding the baby. Fay looked down warmly at the child in her arms. Then she looked up at each of her friends and gave a tiny nod.

"Wonderful," said Essie. "So, obviously we need to do at least what we did yesterday and manage to feed and change the baby. If you three can help me in those duties, I'd also like to do some investigating to try to track down Maria or her husband. Santos has been attempting to contact Maria but he's so new to this country that I'm not sure he knows how to look for someone. Also, he just doesn't have the time to spend on this if he wants to keep his job. We have to help him."

"Of course, we can help!" announced Marjorie for the group. "What should we do first?"

"I'm guessing food will come first," replied Essie. "I fed Antonio just before you three arrived . . . ."

"We fixed another bottle for him with my generic stuff while you were gone," said Opal. "When he's hungry, we're ready."

"Marvelous marbles!" cried Essie in glee. "Marjorie and Fay, maybe you two can figure out a new outfit for Antonio."

"I know what you mean, Essie," said Marjorie. "The little shirt he has on is filthy!" At that, Fay's eyes lit up and she raised her hand in the air.

"Fay?" asked Essie, wondering what the quiet little woman was trying to say. Fay pointed to Antonio's shirt and carefully handed the baby over to Marjorie. Then she pressed the button on the wheelchair arm and headed out Essie's front door with a wave.

"Good Gertrude!" exclaimed Essie, "I wonder if she intends to go shopping for baby clothes. Anyway, Marjorie, Antonio is your charge for now. I'm going to do some telephoning."

As the three remaining women attended to their appointed tasks, the public address system crackled to life. A young woman's gentle voice spoke soothingly.

"Residents, we will be doing our quarterly bug spraying this morning. The exterminators will be by your apartments during the next few hours. You may wish to vacate your apartments for a few hours after the spraying, particularly if you are sensitive to chemicals."

"What?" screamed Essie. "No! Not now! We can't have some bug man in here! What will we do with Antonio?"

"Calm down, Essie," said Opal from the kitchen where she was getting the glove bottle ready. "When he gets here, we'll just slip Antonio in your walker basket and take him for a walk."

"Opal," cried Marjorie, "you aren't thinking of taking him outdoor, are you? He'd freeze!"

"No!" responded Essie, sitting at her desk with her telephone in her hand. "Oh, leaping lobotomies! We don't need this distraction now!"

"We can handle it, Essie," replied Opal. "It's three of us to one poor exterminator!"

"Not a match!" said Marjorie in response. Essie smirked at her friends and continued running her finger down the columns of building construction companies in the business pages of her telephone book. "What are you looking for, Essie?"

"I'm trying to find Antonio's mother," Essie replied, now using her desk-top magnifying glass to read the extremely small print in the large phone book. "Santos said Maria's husband, Gerald Compton, works for a building company that is somehow connected to flowers."

"Can't you just call him at home?" asked Opal, bringing over a filled glove bottle and handing it to

Marjorie who quickly began feeding Antonio. The baby gurgled and began slurping hungrily on the plastic finger. Opal edged herself onto the sofa next to Marjorie, her walker beside Marjorie's.

"I don't think that's wise," explained Essie. "If he's there, it might infuriate him if he thinks I'm involved with this whole mess. If he's not there, I learn nothing. However, if I can find where he works, I might be able to extract some information about him, if I'm careful."

"You mean, if you lie," suggested Marjorie with a wiggle of her pert little nose. She quickly covered Antonio's tiny ears as if to prevent him from hearing the women plot and plan.

"There's nothing I can see that involves flowers and home construction," Essie mused as she read out loud. "I thought maybe they constructed greenhouses or something. Maybe . . . oh! Wait a minute! Rose Brothers' Construction! What do you think?"

"That's probably what Santos meant," agreed Opal. "Are there any other companies with flowers in the titles?"

"Let's see," replied Essie, "Taylor, Unlimited, Willamette . . . no, that appears to be all of the local construction companies. Rose Brothers seems to be the only company that has a flower in its name."

"Call it, Essie!" urged Marjorie, tapping at the directory.

"Yes, give it a try, Essie," seconded Opal. The two friends peered at their friend as Essie noted the number from the book. With a deep breath, she tapped each number on her phone carefully and then waited patiently for an answer. Soon, she was rewarded.

"Oh, yes," said Essie in her most gracious voice into the telephone receiver. "I'm trying to locate one of your employees. Uh . . . I believe he may have left his wallet at my home the other day when he was working on a project here. His name is Gerald Compton . . . according to his driver's license." Essie said this last part slowly as if she were reading the name from an actual driver's license. When the operator evidently responded positively, Essie beamed.

"Oh, wonderful!" she cried. "Mr. Compton works there! Could I speak to him, please?" Essie nodded at her friends on her sofa. Marjorie and Opal smiled in return. Essie listened to the operator and then her face fell. "Oh, no! Oh! Really? Oh, dear! Yes, I understand. Well, I'll call back." She hung up abruptly.

"What happened?" asked Opal.

"It seems," Essie reported, "that Gerald Compton didn't report to work today–as scheduled. The receptionist didn't know where he was."

"Oh, no!" cried Marjorie, "Do you think he has taken Maria and run off somewhere?"

"I don't know," replied Essie with a look of extreme worry. "But this is not a good development. I need to let Santos know that Gerald Compton has apparently disappeared along with Maria. If we don't figure out what has happened to Antonio's mother soon, we'll have to report him to social services . . . abusive father or not."

"We can't do that, Essie!" cried Marjorie, clutching the baby to her breast. "Please, let's try harder. I can't bear the thought of someone hurting this little boy." She placed a tender kiss on the baby's head.

"Me either," agreed Opal, looking down at the baby beside her and gently rubbing his forehead with her finger tips while he drank his formula.

"I certainly know why I like the two of you," said Essie with a sigh. At that moment, Essie's front door opened suddenly. All three women gasped, but were immediately calmed when Fay drove inside in her wheelchair, shutting the front door quickly behind her. Fay motored over to her friends and held up a collection of tiny baby clothes.

Fay smiled as she held up each item of clothing. The women looked at each other and at Fay.

"I don't want to speculate just what Fay is doing with a collection of doll clothes," said Essie, "but these do appear to be about the right size. Although, I'd prefer to avoid using the ruffled pink pinafore even if Antonio couldn't complain about it."

"The little sailor trousers and top are cute!" said Marjorie as she held up each item.

"And she has several onesies," added Opal. "These will be very practical and totally non-sexist." The women sorted through the doll clothes and selected ones right for the baby. Marjorie quickly dressed him in a blue and yellow onesie that covered his small naked feet. Once clothed in his new outfit, the baby looked warm and cozy. As Opal took the rubber glove that Antonio had just finished back to the kitchen, Marjorie placed the baby in her walker basket and she and Opal headed into Essie's bedroom to change what would soon no doubt be a dirty diaper. Essie continued to peruse the telephone book and Fay, left to her own devices, picked up the remote for Essie's television and turned it on.

"This just in," said an announcer's voice, "local authorities have just released the name of the individual killed in that multi-car crash outside of Reardon last night on Highway 79. Sherriff's Office officials say Gerald Compton, age 35 of Reardon, was killed instantly when his car rammed into another vehicle around 6:00 p.m. last night. The driver of the other vehicle remains in serious condition in a local hospital, name withheld pending notification of next of kin." The camera focused on a white sedan butted up against a large tree, its entire front end totally caved in.

"Goggles and galoshes!" shouted Essie, bringing Opal and Marjorie back into the living room with a newly outfitted baby, awake and cheerfully cooing in the basket of Marjorie's walker basket.

"What is it?" called out Opal. "We could hear you scream from all the way in your bathroom."

"It's Antonio's father," said Essie, "he's dead!"

"Oh, no!" cried Marjorie.

"Oh, no!" echoed Opal.

Just then there was a knock on Essie's door and a voice outside called out, "Exterminator, Ma'am!"

Chapter Ten

"There is nothing more concrete than dealing with babies, burps and bottles, frogs and mud."
–Jeane Kirkpatrick

"What should we do?" whispered Essie to her friends.

"Stall him, Essie," said Opal, as the three women quickly wrapped the baby tightly in his blankets and tucked him inside Marjorie's walker basket. Essie rolled over to her front door and spoke through a crack, "Just a minute, please."

"Okay, let him in," said Marjorie, as Essie opened the front door revealing a young man in overalls carrying a large metal canister attached to a spray nozzle.

"Here to spray, Ma'am," he announced.

"Fine," replied Essie, "it's all yours! We're taking a walk."

"Yes, Ma'am," replied the man, as a line of elderly ladies stormed out of the apartment with their vehicles single file, all providing him with gracious cheesy smiles as they departed.

Essie led her little troupe of elderly babysitters through the family room and down a back hallway. As she passed each open doorway, she checked to see if there were any empty locations where the four women could park for a while and contemplate their next moves–and also where they might safely bring little baby Antonio out of his basket prison.

Eventually Essie ducked into an open doorway about halfway down the back hall. Opal, Marjorie, and Fay followed in behind her. This was the Happy Haven Chapel. It only consisted of about eight pews and an altar which was really just a table with a large bronze cross on it. The best thing about the chapel, thought Essie, was the windows. Unlike most of the windows at Happy Haven, these windows were tinted in delicate pastel shades and abstract designs. They really didn't portray much religious symbolism, but they gave a wonderful feeling of calmness and warmth to the small room. Many times, Essie had come into the chapel just to think or reflect or . . . communicate with God. Some people called that praying, but Essie had her own way of describing things.

Essie moved quickly to behind the last row of pews where Marjorie and Opal gathered near her. Fay gently pushed the chapel door shut and joined them, their walkers and her wheelchair circled together like a group of pioneers in a wagon train. Marjorie carefully opened the lid of her basket to discover that baby Antonio was fast asleep.

"If that chapel door opens, Marjorie . . . ." warned Essie, shaking her finger.

"Don't worry, Essie," responded Marjorie in a whisper. "I'm getting good at this."

"We all are," added Opal. She pulled her jacket tighter and shivered. The chapel might look warm but it certainly didn't feel it. "Now, Essie, what next? Do we have to cool our heels here in the chapel for hours until the bug man is finished spraying your apartment?"

"We could go to my place," suggested Marjorie. "It's warmer." She rubbed her hands together and blew into them.

"No!" replied Essie. "It won't be long. Let's keep this close to home. I don't want to chance having Antonio being moved too far from home base...."

"Your apartment being home base!" said Opal with a huff.

"It's not that, Opal!" argued Essie. "I just need to stay close to my room in case Santos comes looking for me. I told him to come tell me the minute he had any new information."

"And you don't think the fact that the baby's father was killed in a car wreck is new information?" asked Marjorie.

"It is!" agreed Essie. "Can you three stay here with Antonio while I go back to the kitchen and let Santos know? He probably has no idea about the accident and that Gerald Compton is dead! This changes everything!"

"Maybe for the good!" added Marjorie, stomping back and forth from one foot to another to warm her feet. "At least that brute can't hurt this baby now!

Excuse me Lord for speaking ill of the dead." She looked up at the chapel ceiling and crossed herself.

"True!" said Essie. "Now that Gerald is dead and out of the picture, maybe Maria, the mother, will come back for baby Antonio and we can return him to where he rightfully belongs!"

"From your lips to God's ears!" added Opal, peering over at the altar.

"What are you waiting for, Essie?" asked Marjorie. "Get going! We'll stay here with the baby. And try to stay warm. If anyone comes in, we'll just say we're . . . ."

"We'll say we're conducting a group prayer session," suggested Opal, with a flourish of her hands like an orchestra conductor. Fay and Marjorie nodded appreciatively at this suggestion and Essie turned her walker and headed out of the chapel.

She zoomed back down the hallway and through the family room and lobby. Luckily, no one appeared to be in the lobby at this time except Phyllis, the front desk clerk, who was manning her station by the front door. Essie waved a greeting as she wheeled by. Phyllis responded with a cheerful 'hello.'

"Merry Christmas, Essie!" she called out as Essie whizzed by towards the dining hall.

"Merry Christmas, Phyllis!" replied Essie, wiggling her fingers quickly at the clerk.

"Don't forget the carolers this afternoon, Essie!" yelled Phyllis at Essie's back. "They're going to be wonderful!"

"Yes! Yes!" replied Essie as she rolled into the dining hall.

Pushing her walker quickly around the empty tables and through the deserted room, Essie rolled to the kitchen entrance and came to a halt. She stood looking into the kitchen, wondering if she should just enter on her own or wait until one of the workers came out so she could ask to speak to Santos. Unable to decide, she moved over to her regular table and sat at her regular spot.

Within a few minutes, Santos appeared at her side.

"Miss Essie!" he cried. "Where is baby?"

"Stop fretting, Santos," replied Essie. "I told you Opal and Marjorie and Fay are watching him. I came back here to see if you had heard the news about Gerald Compton?"

"No, Miss Essie," replied the young man, "What news?"

"It was on the television just a bit ago," she said. "Gerald Compton was in a car crash last night! He's dead, Santos!"

"Oh, Madre Dios!" exclaimed Santos. "How is Maria? Was she with Gerald?"

"The news report did not mention Maria," replied Essie. "Apparently, Gerald was driving alone in his car and was in a multi-car collision. The reporter said there was another victim in another car who was in the hospital but no names were given."

"I cannot believe Maria would be with Gerald in his car," offered Santos. "Maria try to get far away from Gerald! I do not understand, Miss Essie. Where is Maria? If Gerald is dead, where is Maria? Why she not come to get Antonio?"

"That's what I want to know too," said Essie. "Do you think Maria has left town? Maybe she doesn't know about Gerald. Maybe she hasn't heard that he's dead. Could she be the driver of the other car?"

"Maria cannot drive," explained Santos. "She walks to work every day. " He stood forlornly in front of her twisting a dish towel in his hands as he contemplated the whereabouts of his friend.

"Can you think of anywhere she might be? Anyone she might contact? Anyone she would trust?"

"No, Miss Essie, no!"

Essie became quiet. She heaved a loud sigh and stared at her lap. Santos gripped his towel and slowly edged himself into the seat beside her. It was not acceptable behavior for the kitchen staff to sit at the residents' tables, but neither Essie nor the young man next to her were particularly concerned about propriety at the moment. Looks of despair covered both of their faces.

"Santos," said Essie eventually, glancing over at the young man in his starched white uniform, perched on the edge of the chair next to hers, "we simply can't wait indefinitely for Maria to return. The baby's father is dead. His mother is nowhere to be found. We have a moral–no actually–we have a legal obligation to turn this baby over to social services." She gently placed her hand on top of Santos' left hand which was clutching the edge of the table.

Santos's eyes filled with tears as he looked back into Essie's eyes.

"Please, Miss Essie," he begged, "Please, not yet! We must find Maria!" He grabbed Essie's hand with his and squeezed it. If anyone had been watching the two sitting there in the Happy Haven dining hall, they might have thought that they were witnessing a romantic tryst between an older woman and her much younger suitor. Santos squeezed Essie's hand again. "Please!"

"All right," replied Essie, removing her hand from his grasp. "I will try to find Maria. Maybe I can find out where she is and get her to come back for Antonio before we have to report him. Can you think of any place where she might be hiding? Or where she might have gone?"

"No, Miss Essie," said Santos. "I try and think and think where Maria go. Maybe Gerald hurt Maria before he is killed in car accident. Maybe Gerald . . . he, how you say? Encerró . . . lock up Maria."

"You think Maria might be at her home and unable to answer her phone?" asked Essie.

"I do not know," said Santos. "But Maria's apartment is very close to Happy Haven. I will go to Maria's apartment now and see if she is there. I know where Maria keeps key. Maria says Gerald keeps a . . . llave de repuesto . . . a . . . how you say? Spore key?"

"You mean a spare key?"

"Si! Spare key! He keeps spare key under the felpudo . . . is in front of door?"

"Door mat?" guessed Essie. She was becoming a good translator.

"Si," replied Santos, "I get the key and look inside apartment. Maybe Maria is inside and cannot go to the telephone."

"That's a good idea," replied Essie. "At least you won't have to worry about her husband being there."

"Si," agreed Santos. "I am sorry, Miss Essie, to say this to you, but I am not sorry Gerald is dead."

"Given what that man did to that baby and to his wife," replied Essie, "neither am I." She patted Santos's hand and stood up. "I'm going back to check on Antonio now." She smiled encouragingly at the young man and then rolled out of the dining hall.

Chapter Eleven
"A child's life is like a piece of paper on which every passerby leaves a mark."
–Chinese Proverb

Back in the cold chapel, Essie found her three friends playing with baby Antonio. Fay had him on her lap, tightly wrapped in his blankets, gently bouncing him up and down. Antonio seemed to enjoy the attention and the motion, and he responded with soft noises.

"What did you find out, Essie?" asked Opal, as Essie carefully shut the chapel door and rolled toward the group gathered around the baby.

"Santos hasn't heard from Maria," replied Essie, "but he knows where she lives and where the front door key is. He's going to slip out the minute he gets a chance and go over and see if Maria is in her apartment."

"Maybe she's hurt," suggested Marjorie who was sitting on her walker, shivering.

"Yes," added Opal, also on her walker, clutching her palms together in an attempt to warm her hands. "Maybe that husband of hers got drunk and beat her up and then stormed out . . . ."

"And plowed right into another car," added Marjorie.

"That's all possible," replied Essie with a shrug, "but it's all just hypothetical until we find Maria. So far, no one knows where she is. Maybe she doesn't even know that Gerald is dead."

"If she knew he was dead," said Opal, "you'd think she'd return for Antonio. There's nothing to prevent her from keeping her baby now."

"I'm not so sure," said Essie, as she turned her own walker around and sat on her leather seat and chewed on her lip. "Maria is new to this country. Who knows what she knows or thinks? Who knows what garbage her husband filled her head with?"

"True," agreed Marjorie. "If that Gerald tried to convince her that he could take her baby from her or send her back to Mexico or any other crazy thing, that poor woman could be hiding . . . even if she does know her husband is dead. Maybe she thinks that Antonio is safer with Santos."

"It's hard to know," said Essie, nodding to Marjorie's thoughts. She looked over at Fay who was having a quiet private conversation with baby Antonio and was apparently oblivious to the discussion the other women were having. She wondered if Fay was at all aware of the serious situation that the child she held was in. It didn't appear so. It only appeared that Fay and Antonio were having a delightful time in their own little world. Fay cradled the baby in her arms and pushed the button on her wheelchair. The device moved soundlessly forward and Fay glided around the outside of the chapel slowly, giving Antonio a ride and pointing to all the sparkly sunbeams that pierced through the stained glass windows.

"I think we can probably return to my place," said Essie to Opal and Marjorie. "It's been at least an hour since the bug man sprayed." She glanced at her wrist watch.

"Yes," agreed Marjorie, "and we need to get back before Antonio starts to get hungry."

"Which could be anytime," added Opal. "He's a greedy little Gus when it comes to his protein drink."

"Let's go, then. It's freezing in here!" said Essie, rising and grabbing her walker handlebars. "Fay, come on! We're going back to my place! Bring the baby here so we can tuck him back into his basket!" Fay responded quickly and moved her wheelchair back to the three women. She carefully wrapped Antonio's blankets tighter and handed him to Essie.

"Come on, little papoose!" said Essie to the baby. "Back you go into your carriage! Sorry we have to hide you like this."

"I think he likes his basket, Essie," said Marjorie, "At least, he never cries when he's in there."

"You're right," said Essie. "It's probably the motion."

"That's surely it," agreed Opal. The women tucked the infant inside the basket and gently closed the lid. Then with Essie in the lead, they headed out of the chapel and down the back hallway, through the family room, and into Essie's hallway.

As they passed through the empty family room, they noticed a commotion in the lobby, directly in front of the front desk. One of the residents was sitting on the ground surrounded by staff and other residents. A nurse was positioned at the woman's head, her arm around the resident's shoulders. All of a sudden, the woman bent forward and heaved her breakfast onto the ground. All the residents standing around moved back cautiously. The staff nurse cradled the woman and helped her lie down. She gestured for one of the staff to go and the young man headed out of the lobby. Essie saw all of this activity with a sideways glance as she led her three friends through the family room and down her hallway.

When they reached Essie's apartment, Essie motioned for them to remain at the doorway as she entered on her own. She walked around inside, sniffing. When she returned to the doorway, she gave the "okay" signal and the three friends entered Essie's front door. Fay quickly removed the baby from the basket and motored over to the window with him.

"I think the bug spray odor has dissipated enough, don't you?" she asked.

"I can't say, Essie," said Opal. "My sense of smell isn't what it used to be. But I still smell something."

"Me too," added Marjorie.

"Well, we're going to have to put up with it," noted Essie. "At least it's warm in here. Wait a minute! I have an idea." She rummaged around in her desk drawer and brought out a small metal spray bottle wrapped in gleaming gold foil. "Here! This should do the trick! It's Christmas incense! I won it at Bingo the other night. It has frankincense and myrrh in it." She unwrapped the sprayer and pushed the atomizer on the top of the device. Suddenly a heavenly aroma began to permeate the room. "Doesn't it smell good?"

"If you say so, Essie," said Marjorie.

"Yes, Essie, I trust your judgment on smell-related topics," said Opal.

"What!" exclaimed Essie, placing the sprayer back on the top of her desk. "You mean you two can't smell all those lovely middle eastern odors wafting around in here?"

"Not really," admitted Marjorie with a sheepish grin.

"Me neither," said Opal. "Is it important?"

"What about you, Fay?" Essie asked her plump friend who had stationed herself by the window where she was showing Antonio the snowflakes that were drifting down outside. Fay turned to Essie when she heard her name called. "Can you smell the frankincense?"

Fay took a deep breath, smiled and nodded several times. Then she returned her attention to the baby.

"There!" said Essie to Opal and Marjorie, "There's someone else with a delicate sense of smell, just like me!"

"My sense of smell is good enough to register when Antonio has filled his britches," cried Marjorie.

"Mine too!" added Opal. "Besides, Essie, what any of us can or can't smell is totally beside the point. We need to get Antonio's glove ready for his next feeding."

"You're right," said Essie, reluctantly. Even so, she rolled around the room and sprayed the holiday scent all around her living room. Opal and Marjorie headed to the kitchen where they began to prepare a new batch of Vigor formula in Antonio's glove bottle.

"Did anyone see who that was on the floor in the lobby when we passed through?" asked Essie.

"It looked like Adele Anderson," said Marjorie, "but I'm not sure. Poor thing! Do you think she got food poisoning?"

"She was certainly heaving her meal," noted Opal with a certain amount of disgust.

"I saw a resident vomit this morning in the dining hall," added Essie, "when I was down talking to Santos."

"Maybe it's bad broccoli," offered Marjorie. "There was an outbreak of a bad batch of that several weeks ago. It was on the news. Remember?"

"I do," agreed Opal, standing next to Marjorie while they filled the glove, "but that was in Arizona. There was never a report of any bad broccoli here."

"Luckily," said Essie to them as she sat in her lounge chair and picked up her telephone book, "Antonio doesn't eat broccoli. So, I think we're okay."

"You mean, Antonio's okay, Essie," replied Opal, primly. "We would only be okay if we didn't eat any of the tainted broccoli."

"Now, Opal," argued Marjorie, "This is all hypothetical. We don't know that there's any bad broccoli around. We don't even know if Adele has food poisoning. Let's just remain calm and not exaggerate."

"Yes," agreed Essie from her chair, "Let's concentrate on Antonio . . . and finding his mother."

At that point, Essie's telephone rang.

"Oh, no!" said Essie. "No one ever calls me!" She allowed the device to continue ringing.

"Essie," said Marjorie, wheeling herself over to Essie's side from the kitchen. "You can't just not answer the phone." Opal followed behind, gesturing for Essie to answer. She handed the glove bottle to Fay then rolled back to Essie.

"It might be about Antonio," Opal said, motioning for Essie to answer, "or about his mother. Answer it, Essie."

"That's ridiculous!" said Essie on the third ring, "No one knows I'm involved in looking for Antonio's mother . . . at least no one who knows my telephone number."

"Santos knows," said Marjorie. Marjorie and Opal hovered beside Essie's chair, encouraging her to answer the phone as they might encourage someone to capture a poisonous snake that was slithering around loose on the floor.

"But he's . . . ," said Essie on ring number four. "Oh, maybe it is Santos. But he doesn't know my telephone number."

"Essie, answer the phone!" cried Opal. With a deep sigh, Essie cautiously removed the receiver and carefully put it to her ear.

"Hello," she said in a tiny voice. She listened a bit then responded, smiling. "Oh, Claudia, dear. Hello." Placing a hand over the mouthpiece, she whispered to the other women, "It's my youngest daughter." Then, returning to the telephone, she continued to listen to her child's voice on the other end. Soon, her face began to change from a warm expression to one of concern. "But, dear," she interjected to the unseen Claudia on the telephone, "I really don't think I'm up for all that!"

"What, Essie?" asked Opal, pushing in front of Marjorie so she could whisper in Essie's ear and nudging her arm. Marjorie shoved Opal out of the way and moved closer to the phone too so she might be able to hear what Essie's adult daughter was suggesting that was possibly going to cause a problem for the four elderly babysitters.

"Don't tell her about the . . . you-know-who," whispered Marjorie in Essie's ear. Essie waved her hand at Marjorie and Opal and then cupped it over the ear piece in an effort to drown out the distracting voices in the room. Fay remained blissfully unaware (it seemed) of the little drama taking place around Essie's telephone as she fed baby Antonio from the glove bottle.

"Yes, dear," replied Essie to her daughter, "Yes, I heard about the carolers, but I really wasn't planning on trekking down to hear them. I can usually hear them in my room. They're always fairly loud." Essie smiled at Marjorie and Opal who both appeared to catch on immediately to what Claudia was apparently suggesting to Essie on the telephone. They scowled in unison as they watched their friend use her charm to finagle her way out of an obvious invitation from her daughter. "Yes, dear," continued Essie into the receiver, "I'm thrilled that Kurt has arrived early. Yes, it's lovely that the three of you want to take me out to dinner and come over to listen to the carolers with me this afternoon . . . ."

Marjorie and Opal responded with wide eyes and open mouths when Essie paraphrased her daughter's invitation. Obviously, the last thing Essie needed was to have her attention diverted from solving the problem of finding Antonio's mother by having to entertain her three adult children at a Christmas music festival followed by a dinner out. Marjorie began to gesture to Essie in an attempt to offer a suggestion. Opal, with a competing suggestion in mind, restrained Marjorie's hands with hers and also tried to get Essie's attention. Fay continued to feed the baby and smile.

"But, dear!" cried Essie into the phone, "I'm just not up for going out to dinner today!"

Opal and Marjorie nodded vociferously when they heard Essie's latest excuse. Obviously, if an elderly lady is not up to an outing, she is not up to it. Surely, that would be the end of it. The two women waited frozen for Essie to seal the deal.

"But, Claudia!" exclaimed Essie, "Please!" Essie listened a bit longer and then heaved a huge sigh. "Yes, dear," she intoned morosely into the phone, "I'll see you at four." She slowly placed the receiver back on the phone.

"Essie!" cried Marjorie, stomping her foot, "you can't go out! You can't have your children over here!" She stood up straight at her walker and placed her hands emphatically on her hips.

"What about Antonio, Essie?" added Opal, pulling herself up to her full imposing height and expanding her chest. She towered over Essie in her lounge chair. "What about the baby?"

"I'm sorry, girls," replied Essie, a bit sheepishly, "but my Claudia simply will not take no for an answer. It seems my son Kurt has arrived in town early for Christmas and now that all three children are here they want to take me out to dinner . . . and to the caroling concert this afternoon. What can I say? Claudia says the three of them will be here at four and she's not taking no for an answer. And she won't. She's stubborn."

"You're her mother, Essie!" exclaimed Opal, her long, thin face awash with turmoil. "Just tell her to stay home!"

"Just tell her you're not going," said Marjorie, in her cheerful but insistent school teacher voice. "Can't you claim your arthritis is acting up, or something?"

"She'd know that was a lie," replied Essie with a grimace. "I never let things like arthritis get in my way."

"That's true," agreed Opal. "You're as stubborn as your daughter, Essie." The four women sat quietly in a circle for several minutes. The only sound was the occasional coo of a small baby. Eventually, Essie stood up.

"I'm not just going to sit here," said Essie, finally, with bravado. "I've got hours before my children arrive. There's plenty we can do to find Antonio's mother before then. And then . . . if we haven't found her . . . you three can take the baby to one of your rooms until I return from my dinner out. What do you say?"

"Okay," replied the others enthusiastically. Actually, Fay just nodded.

108 *Papoosed*

Chapter Twelve

"The hand that rocks the cradle is the hand that rules the world."
–William Ross Wallace

When baby Antonio had finally drifted off to sleep for his mid-morning nap, the women parted company and each returned to their own rooms for a while. Essie zipped out to the Happy Haven family room and surreptitiously grabbed a copy of the morning newspaper which had been tossed haphazardly in sections on one of the square card tables in the middle of the room. She glanced around to make sure that no one observed her making off with the paper. Residents were expected to read the newspaper in the family room and then leave it there—in good condition—for other residents to read. Essie ignored this stipulation, slipped the paper into her basket and rolled quickly back down her hallway and into her room. She peeked into her bedroom to make sure that Antonio was still asleep—which he was—and then, she plopped herself down in her comfortable lounge chair and withdrew the newspaper from her walker's basket.

Quickly she scanned the pages, looking for anything that might provide more information about Gerald Compton's fatal accident the day before. She knew that local newspapers invariably provided more detailed reports of events that occurred in their area than did local television stations. It was simply a matter of logistics, she reasoned. The television news programs only had a half hour to present the most important, or as Essie often thought, the most salacious, details. Newspapers could get to the deeper aspects of a story. Using her handheld magnifying glass, Essie's eyes went up and down the columns in Reardon's small daily paper. Towards the end of the first section, she found a story headlined, "Multi-car collision claims life of local resident." She immediately began reading the contents of the article, searching for any tidbit that might not have been presented in the television report of the crash. Here she learned again that Gerald Compton was 35. He had worked at Rose Brothers' Construction. His address was given and she recognized the street as one she knew that was close to Happy Haven, which made sense because Santos had said that Maria walked to work. The article claimed that Gerald Compton was a life-long resident of Reardon and was survived by his father. What? She re-read the last line. What about his wife? Quickly scanning the article, she realized that Gerald's wife Maria was not even mentioned. That was strange. What did that mean? Did the reporter just do a shoddy job of checking the facts about Gerald or—worse—could it be that Gerald and Maria were not legally married? If that was the case, the situation for baby Antonio was even more precarious—his citizenship status definitely in question. She would have to be extremely cautious to protect the little fellow until she could find his mother and determine what was going on. If Antonio was discovered and his mother was not, it would very likely mean that he'd be put in a foster home.

    She listened for Antonio, but the baby made no sound. Luckily, it appeared that he was not bothered by all the drama going on around him, all of which affected him so directly. Essie re-read the newspaper article. She contemplated the information about Gerald Compton being listed as a life-long resident of Reardon and his only relative being his father. She tried to imagine how this information would have come to light. Gerald Compton had been in a fatal car crash. When this occurred, the police probably looked for identification on him—or in his car—and that information somehow led them to Gerald's father, not to Maria. Essie reasoned that Gerald must not have had any identifying material on himself or in his car that even mentioned his wife, Maria, but that somehow did mention his father. Possibly, she mused, Gerald was driving his father's car. If that were the case, the police would immediately contact the father and report to him that Gerald had been killed in the car.

    "Yes," said Essie to herself. "That's quite likely. Maybe the father had an old clunker and was letting his son drive it—particularly if the son couldn't afford a car of his own. Gerald did have a job at Rose Brothers' Construction," she remembered. "Maybe there was some information on Gerald or in the car that led the police to Rose Brothers' Construction and someone who knew him there directed the police to Gerald's father. There were various possibilities."

Essie scowled and stood up and rolled her walker over to her outside window. The snow had stopped falling and a layer of white several inches thick was now glistening on the ground. The bright sunlight made the scene directly outside of Essie's window sparkle like an icy wonderland. She imagined baby Antonio all dressed up in a bright red snowsuit being pulled on a little wooden sled, laughing his chubby little cheeks off. She tapped her fingers on her handlebars as she tried to imagine what might have happened last night that led to the fateful death of Gerald Compton and the disappearance of his wife Maria. She needed more information, she realized.

Quickly, she rolled back and sat in her lounge chair and pulled out her telephone book. Using her magnifying glass again, she turned to the yellow pages and looked under "Newspapers." It infuriated her that the telephone company always produced their books with such small print. Holding her glass over the column of local papers, she moved it down the column until she located the one she sought—Reardon Daily Times. Then, with her index finger pointed directly at the target telephone number, she grabbed her telephone receiver and punched in the digits.

"Hello," she said when an operator answered with, "Reardon Daily Times. How may I direct your call?"

"I'd like to speak to one of your reporters, please. A Bernice McVickers?" Essie moved her index finger from the telephone number to the byline of the reporter above the newspaper article that had reported Gerald Compton's death.

"One moment," replied the efficient operator, "I'll connect you to that office."

Hmm, thought Essie, as she waited to speak to the reporter. She had never spoken to an actual newspaper reporter before. The idea of it was somewhat daunting and a little bit exciting.

"Watts here," said a male voice in her ear.

"Excuse me," replied Essie to the man. "I'm looking for Bernice McVickers."

"Not here today," replied the man curtly. "This is Don Watts. Can I help?"

"I . . . uh . . . don't know," answered Essie. "I wanted to talk to her about the article she wrote about that multi-car accident that occurred last night."

"Oh, yeah," interjected the male voice, "That was a bad one! The guy really rammed that other car. Going about eighty, police thought. Oops, sorry. You a relative?"

"Uh, no," said Essie, now wondering if she could possibly extract any information from this reporter. "I . . . uh, live in the area . . ." She reasoned that was not a total fabrication as she did live maybe ten or so blocks from where the accident occurred. ". . . and I was worried about the safety of . . . the location."

"Oh, lady," replied the man, "I know that corner. From what Bernice was saying the other day here in the office, it was totally the dead guy's fault. Not to speak ill of the . . . you know . . . but he must have been drunk or something. The guy in the other car is lucky to be alive."

"It was a guy . . . a man . . . in the other car?" she asked.

"Yeah," he said, "but I don't think the police have released that yet. Still trying to track down next of kin. Hey, but if you live around there, you know that corner has a stop sign. I wouldn't worry if I were you."

"Yes, thank you," she replied. "Uh, when will Miss McVickers be in?"

"Probably not till tomorrow," he said casually, "but with Bernice you never know. Depends on the story." He chuckled.

"Yes, well, I may try to call her then," said Essie, "Uh, thank you, Mr., uh, Don."

The man said, "Yup," and hung up without another word.

"Oh, dear," said Essie. "That was no help at all. Well, maybe a bit of help. At least I know Maria wasn't in either of the cars involved in that crash. So, where is she? What happened last night after she dropped that baby off in the Happy Haven kitchen?" She drummed her fingers on the open phone book.

After a thoughtful pause, she quickly thumbed through the yellow pages and again found the number for the Rose Brothers' Construction Company that she had dialed earlier. She touched each number on her phone and listened as the number rang at Rose Brothers.

"Rose Brothers' Construction," said a pleasant female voice.

"Yes," said Essie. "I'm sorry to bother you. This may seem like an odd request . . ."

The receptionist chuckled. "Excuse me," she said, "but we get a lot of odd requests. Just yesterday, someone wanted us to actually build an outhouse! Can you believe it? In this day and age, with indoor plumbing? Why would anyone want to actually construct an outhouse?"

Essie was warming to the woman who seemed so willing to share private information with a casual caller. Possibly she would share the information that Essie needed.

"That is strange," agreed Essie, in an attempt to ingratiate herself with the operator. "So, I guess my request won't seem so unusual then. I'm trying to find out about one of your employees who, I understand, died recently . . . a Gerald Compton."

"That's Harold's son!" exclaimed the woman. "It's just horrible! Did you know Gerald? Harold is just broken up!"

"Yes, I can imagine that he is," said Essie, digesting this additional information. "And what about Gerald's wife?"

"Wife?" cried the voice on the phone. "Gerald didn't have a wife! Oh, you mean that woman he met in Mexico?"

"Yes," said Essie, "I understand that they were married in Mexico . . ."

"Harold is furious about her! He always told Gerald that that woman was just using him to get her green card! I'm not supposed to know," she whispered to Essie. "I just work the desk, but I heard Harold and Gerald going at it a number of times about that woman. Harold blames her for all of Gerald's problems, I think."

"Why would he blame her?"

"I don't know, ma'am," responded the woman on the phone, "I just know Harold and his son were always fighting about her. Mr. Rose said Harold wouldn't be in today . . . because of Gerald being killed in the accident. Everybody here is pretty shook up."

"You mean they all liked Gerald?"

"Oh, no," she said in an even softer voice, "nobody liked Gerald . . . or Harold, but, geez they are . . . were really good workers. Mr. Rose would never fire Harold; he's been with the company for years, and Gerald is like a . . . package deal with Harold. Besides, Gerald is a hard worker too. . . was a hard worker."

"Uh, do you by any chance know where this . . . where Gerald's wife is?" asked Essie cautiously, trying to secure the most important piece of information before the operator's patience ran out.

"No, I don't have a clue!" she replied flippantly, "I never saw the woman. Only heard them argue about her. Truthfully, I think she was just a figment of Gerald's imagination."

"Why do you say that?"

"Because Gerald is . . . was . . . a dog," she said with scorn. "No woman in her right mind would marry him. Oh, yeah, he was good lookin' and all, but . . . . Hey, I can't talk anymore. Mr. Rose is heading this way." She hung up abruptly.

Essie pondered the treasure trove of information she had just acquired from the receptionist at Rose Brothers' Construction Company. There was clarity now on some issues. Gerald Compton apparently was the no-good jerk that Maria had told Santos he was. Why had she married him in the first place? Was it just physical attraction? Gerald and his father Harold both worked at Rose Brothers' Construction and neither were liked, although both were hard workers. Gerald and his father had had some heated arguments about a woman . . . apparently Maria, but no one at Rose Brothers seemed to think that Gerald was married. Curious and more curious. However, the major question . . . where was Maria? . . . remained unanswered.

Chapter Thirteen
"I thought I had forgotten how to hold a baby–but my arms remember."
–Author Unknown

Essie was still sitting in her lounger pondering the relationship between Gerald and Maria Compton. She could see through her bedroom door. Baby Antonio was still sleeping soundly. There was a soft knocking on her front door. Essie rose as quickly as her arthritic knees would allow and hastily moved her walker towards the door where she cracked it open a bit.

Outside, Santos stood in his winter jacket, his hand raised to knock again. He was bouncing from one foot to another as he looked cautiously around.

"Jumpin' Juniper!" whispered Essie, "Get in here!" She motioned the young man to enter. Santos followed Essie inside and quietly closed the door behind him. She scooted back to her chair and plopped back down, pointing to her sofa. Santos remained standing.

"I cannot stay, Miss Essie," he said, nervously twisting his hands together. "I must get back to make lunch. Is baby okay?" He looked around Essie's small living room.

"Antonio's fast asleep, Santos," she replied, "on my bed. Do you want to see?" She started to rise. Santos held out his hand to stop her.

"No! No! Miss Essie!" he said quickly, "I must hurry. I go to Maria and Gerald's apartment, like you say. I find key where Maria keeps it. I go inside." He grimaced and panted dramatically.

"What, Santos?" Essie demanded. "What happened?"

"Horrible, Miss Essie!" he exclaimed. "Everything in apartment is all . . . how you say? . . . arrancados . . . ripped! Like there was a big fight!"

"Oh, no!" she cried, patting a spot for Santos on her sofa. The young man cautiously sat on the flowered settee. "Any sign of Maria?"

"I do not see Maria," he replied, "but I find sangre . . . blood . . . on the carpet, Miss Essie!"

"Blood! Why weren't the police there?" she asked, almost to herself. "You'd think the police would attempt to check out the residence of an accident victim . . . hmmm."

"No police, Miss Essie!" said Santos. "But I do find this!" He reached under his jacket and into his side pants' pocket and brought out a small blue wallet. He thrust it at Essie.

"What's this?" she demanded, taking it immediately and opening it. "It's Maria's! This is her green card, Santos! Why would she leave without her purse? Do you remember if she had it when she brought you the baby last night?" She examined the card and the remaining meager contents of the small wallet and then placed it on her end table.

"I do not remember, Miss Essie," he said. "I only think about baby Antonio."

"Yes, yes," she replied. "She must have returned to her apartment after she came here and gave you the baby. She probably had some sort of argument with Gerald then. If she left her purse and identification in her apartment, she probably left in a hurry . . . maybe under threat. Did you see anything else in the apartment, Santos?"

"I . . . I . . . see," he said, closing his eyes squeezing his forehead muscles together in an attempt to recall the scene. "I see Maria's maleta . . . suitcase . . . on bed!"

"She was probably packing . . . getting ready to leave Gerald!" added Essie.

"If Gerald catch her leaving him, he be very mad, Miss Essie!" said Santos.

"It appears that Maria must have escaped," suggested Essie, as the two unlikely sleuths contemplated together the possible events that led to their being responsible for the sleeping baby in the next room.

"Yes, Miss Essie," agreed Santos, "and maybe Gerald, he goes after Maria."

"And in his fury ended up in that fatal accident!"

"Is possible," noted Santos.

"But still conjecture," said Essie, "However, I have some additional information to add that might enlighten the information you've just brought me." She told Santos what she had discovered from the receptionist at the Rose Brothers' Construction Company. The young Hispanic man and the old woman continued to discuss the possible scenarios that might have led to the circumstances of the previous evening.

"All of these are possible," said Essie to Santos, who was still looking forlorn. "But, they don't answer the primary question which is where Maria is. Santos, if we don't find Maria soon . . . and I emphasize soon . . . we will simply have to inform the authorities. If for no other reason than it appears that no one is aware of Maria's disappearance. What if Gerald hurt her and she ran away and then collapsed from her injuries? She could be lying in a ditch somewhere."

"I do not think of that, Miss Essie," replied Santos, now looking even more frightened. "I only worry why Maria not come to get baby. I do not think she is hurt. What we do, Miss Essie?"

"If we report her disappearance to the police . . ." mused Essie.

"No, Miss Essie!" cried Santos. "Please! I promise Maria I not tell authorities. I promise I keep baby Antonio safe till she comes back."

"But when, Santos?" asked Essie. "You didn't promise to watch him indefinitely."

"I do not know what to do," cried Santos, hands rummaging in his pants' pockets.

"Listen," said Essie, bending forward and patting the young man's arm. "I . . . I mean, we . . . will watch baby Antonio. My friends and I . . . we've developed a system, actually, so it's really not a problem. But we can't do this much longer . . . for Antonio's sake, Santos! This baby needs care from a parent not from four old women . . . even if we are four incredibly able old women who were all mothers at one time."

"You wonderful lady, Miss Essie," said Santos warmly, grasping her hand and squeezing it. "You and Miss Opal and Miss Marjorie and Miss Fay. You very nice ladies. You very good mothers one time, I think." He smiled at her.

"Well," she said, shirking her shoulders, "it isn't hard to be a good mother to baby Antonio. He's probably the most easy-going, agreeable infant I've ever encountered. My three children were a lot fussier than he is when they were newborns!" She chuckled and Santos joined her.

"I go now, Miss Essie," he said, starting to rise from the sofa. "I need to get lunch ready for residents of Happy Haven. You come to lunch, Miss Essie?"

"I'll be there some time after my three partners in crime get here to babysit," she said. A soft cry sounded and Essie rose and pushed her walker toward the bedroom. "My charge calls."

Santos remained seated as Essie entered her bedroom. Baby Antonio was awake but apparently entranced with the rays of sunlight bursting through Essie's bedroom window. He had flung his towel blankets off and was moving his arms and legs with gusto. She scooped Antonio up and slipped him into the walker basket and wheeled him back to the living room over to Santos.

"Very happy baby!" said Santos. "Not like father!"

"Yes," agreed Essie. "Here, Santos. You hold your charge for a while." She bent over the handlebars of her walker and pointed to where Santos should place his hands. Carefully, Santos slipped his arms beneath the baby's neck and bottom and scooped him gently into his arms. "You're a natural!"

"Baby smells very good!" announced Santos.

"That's all the creams and powders we've been dousing him with," replied Essie. "Believe me, there are times when he doesn't smell so good!" Santos laughed and rocked Antonio back and forth. The baby stared up at Santos unwaveringly with big dark eyes.

"Talk to him," said Essie.

"Hello, baby Antonio," whispered Santos in a soft voice. "I'm Santos. I am very sorry I cannot find your mama. I try very hard. Miss Essie and friends try very hard. We try to find your mama." He said these words with a sincere intensity that Essie found moving. Obviously the baby could not understand the meaning, but probably could feel the commitment and love from the young man.

"I think he likes you," noted Essie, as baby Antonio made soft noises and moved his head a bit.

Santos and baby continued to bond for a few more precious moments. Then, Santos eventually placed the infant back in Essie's walker basket and rose from her sofa and headed for her door.

"Thank you, Miss Essie," he said, hand on doorknob. "I keep try to find Maria. I talk to you at lunch."

"Yes," she replied, straightening the baby's covers in the basket. "I will keep trying to track her down too, Santos. Maybe something in her little purse will provide a lead. I'll let you know what I find, if anything, at lunch. Please keep your chin up." She tucked the small wallet in her pants' pocket.

"Chin?" asked Santos, suddenly grasping his face. "Is chin down?"

"It's just an expression," replied Essie, smiling at Santos, "It means don't lose hope."

"Santos' chin is very up, Miss Essie!" he said with a jaunty thrust of his chin as he headed out her door.

"Good," replied Essie to herself. "Now, if I can just keep my chin up!"

Chapter Fourteen
"There is nothing in the world of art like the songs mother used to sing."
–Billy Sunday

Essie remained in her room when she would normally go to lunch. Her stomach was rumbling because she hadn't eaten much breakfast. She thought how used to eating at a certain time of day she had become and even having to wait an additional half an hour was making her uncomfortable. Finally, Marjorie, Opal, and Fay arrived at her door, already having rushed through their meals.

"Where is my little papoose?" squealed Marjorie, with a shake of her bouncy curls, when the three women had gathered inside Essie's small living room.

"Yours?" replied Opal with a regal glare at Marjorie, rolling into Essie's kitchen and automatically starting to prepare new glove bottles for Antonio. "Don't you mean ours, Marjorie?"

Essie wheeled her walker into the bedroom to get the baby and quickly returned with the infant in her basket. Fay motored her wheelchair over to Essie and reached in and quickly scooped up Antonio into her lap. She immediately started to cuddle him. As she hummed a soft lullaby the little boy responded with a wide-eyed stare at Fay's face.

"I didn't know Fay could sing," called out Opal from the kitchen.

"She's humming, not singing," replied Marjorie, now seated on the sofa. "Essie, you'd better get going if you want any flounder. It's the special of the day and almost everyone ordered it."

"I don't care what I eat," said Essie, heading for the door, "as long as I get something. You three be careful and keep the noise down. Clara Monroe was complaining to me that she could hear a lot of sound from my place. She thinks I have visitors."

"Did she mention a baby?" asked Opal, looking up at Essie from her formula preparation efforts.

"Yes," replied Essie at the door, "but, I think she just thinks I have an apartment full of guests."

"You do," responded Marjorie with a twinkle in her eye, "three adults and one child! You're a regular motel!"

Essie chuckled, and then shook her finger at her friend.

"It's not funny, Marjorie," she scolded. "Clara is a pest and I wouldn't put it past her to cause trouble for us."

"You're right, Essie," agreed Opal, solemnly, her long, aquiline nose lifted. "We'll be as quiet as possible. But, we can't do much about Antonio. Babies cry. There's not much you can do about that!"

"I know," said Essie, "but try to attend to his needs as soon as possible so he doesn't want to cry!"

"We have Fay for that!" exclaimed Marjorie, totally undeterred by the criticism. "She's a pro at calming babies!" And truly it was so, as all three women glanced at Fay who was engaged in some private silent conversation with Antonio by Essie's outside window.

Essie shrugged and headed out of her apartment and down her hallway. She felt comfortable entrusting Antonio's care to her friends. They all obviously had bonded as much with the little boy as she had. One infant was no match for four old ladies, she reasoned. Even if the relationship had to remain on the Q.T. Essie moved into the family room, around the tall Christmas tree, and into the lobby. As it was lunch time, the lobby was filled with residents and visitors. Some people were sitting and chatting in front of the fireplace. Some were walking through the lobby going in or out of the facility. A line of three or four people stood at the front desk which was at the moment manned by Phyllis who was festively attired in a bright green sweater with red buttons. Phyllis was answering questions from a lady at the head of the line about her mother who apparently was a Happy Haven resident.

"No, ma'am," Phyllis was saying. "I don't know where she might be. You could check the community room upstairs."

"She's usually in her apartment at this time," replied the worried woman.

"She might be in the dining hall having lunch," offered Phyllis, her genuine smile topped by her rich brown eyes.

"No, I checked there," said the woman, now becoming somewhat unnerved.

Essie noted this dialogue as she passed by on her way to the dining hall. She knew that the woman would eventually find her mother because, although Happy Haven was large, there were only so many places where residents could go. It was unlikely that any resident would venture outside for long on a day like today. She glanced out the main double doors of the facility as she rolled on. Snow was not just drifting down, it was now blowing, and she could hear the wind howling even from the lobby. She was glad to be inside and glad that baby Antonio was safe inside, but she couldn't help but worry about the location of the infant's mother. What had happened to her? Had her husband beaten her? Had she run out and gotten lost or fallen and been unable to get to safety? Where could she be? Essie hoped that Maria was not stranded outside in this increasingly foul weather.

As she entered the dining hall, she heard Phyllis now speaking to the next person in line. Their conversation was also about the visitor's mother . . . something about the mother being sick in her room and needing additional care. This was also a common situation and families frequently adjusted a resident's care status when the person's health needs changed.

Essie rolled her walker to her regular table and sat at her spot. It seemed lonely without Opal and Marjorie and Fay. Essie preferred to eat her meals with company, and at this late point in the lunch period, most residents had already finished their meals and had returned to their rooms. She glanced around. Several residents remained at their tables sipping beverages. A waitress quickly brought Essie a menu and she pointed to the flounder, hoping there was still some of the favorite dish remaining. Soon, her meal arrived and she ate quietly. She caught a glimpse of Santos several times and he seemed busy so she refrained from signaling him. Indeed, she had nothing new to report to him so she merely sat and sipped her coffee for a few minutes before she returned to her room.

"Miss Essie," said a male voice. She looked up to see Hubert Darby standing beside her, sporting a new festive vest. Did the man have an outfit for every one of the twelve days of Christmas? "Miss Essie, did you like my present?"

"Oh, Hubert," replied Essie, "that was a lovely thought, but I really can't eat hard candy with my . . . uh . . . dentures, so I haven't actually opened your present yet." She smiled warmly at the man. Maybe if Hubert knew she wore dentures, Essie reasoned, he'd cool his apparent ardor.

"Please, Miss Essie," continued Hubert, evidently undeterred by her dental condition, "please open my gift." He lifted up and down on his heels in a nervous gesture and then abruptly turned and walked purposefully out of the dining hall. Essie shrugged and returned to her coffee. She had barely had a moment of peace when another voice interrupted her meal.

"Essie," said Violet Hendrickson, "I'm glad I ran into you."

Essie stared up at the Happy Haven Director looming over her, armed with a clipboard and pen as if they were weapons.

"Miss Hendrickson," said Essie, cringing. This was not a good situation. Violet had discovered Essie seated in the dining hall, making it difficult for Essie to make a quick getaway as she had the other day when she'd used her weak bladder as an excuse to avoid the director. "So nice to see you."

"Essie," said Violet, glaring over the top of her clipboard, her golden earrings gleaming like armor around her face. "Clara Monroe came to see me, concerned that you are having loud visitors in your apartment."

"What?" sputtered Essie, spilling some of her coffee on her lap. "She actually went and complained to you?" Essie knew Clara was a busybody and a buttinsky but she'd only thought the woman was annoying. Essie didn't really think Clara would go to Violet and make a fuss. Essie assumed Clara was as intimidated by Violet as she–and everybody else at Happy Haven–was. This was not a good development.

"Yes," continued Violet, tapping her pen with a vengeance on her clipboard, "Clara says she can hear a crowd of people in your apartment at all hours of the day and night!"

"Oh, Miss Hendrickson," exclaimed Essie, "that's absolutely not true! I don't know where Clara is getting such ideas!"

"Have you been entertaining a noisy crowd of people in your apartment, Essie?" demanded Violet. Even though Violet's voice was soft, it was insistent, and the few remaining diners had now turned to see what was going on at Essie's table.

"Of course not, Miss Hendrickson!" replied Essie. "Oh, I know what it must be!" she fabricated quickly. "I did have my tablemates over last night. We were . . . uh, working on a surprise present for one of the residents . . . but I don't believe we were terribly loud."

"Clara says she hears many loud voices late at night! Even children! Infants! Have you had relatives staying with you, Essie?" Violet's eyes were like those of a hypnotist's, and Essie could feel herself being drawn into her power. It was not against Happy Haven policy to have overnight guests, but if guests became so rowdy that they disturbed a resident's neighbors, they would be asked to leave.

"Oh, no, Miss Hendrickson!" said Essie, her face becoming red. "All of my relatives live in or near Reardon. There's no need for any of them to spend the night with me!" She looked down at the ground to break the threatening spell that the heartless administrator was weaving.

"No children? No infants?" pushed Violet, stabbing her pencil at Essie.

"I know! My tablemates and I were watching that new reality show last night about the family with twenty children. Can you imagine a woman giving birth to twenty babies? I had three and that was more than enough for me! There were lots of children and infants on the show. That's probably what Clara heard!" Essie laughed pitifully and glanced up over her glasses to see if Violet was buying her story.

"Humph!" said Violet, continuing to tap her pencil on her crossed arms. She fingered one of her gold earrings as if it were a beetle she was contemplating squashing, and took a deep breath. "I don't know what you're up to, Essie Cobb, but mark my word; I'm going to find out!" She said this last part in a whispered snarl. Then, she turned abruptly and stormed out, her high heels clipping on the linoleum floor.

"Sue's gnus!" said Essie to herself. She glanced around and gave a friendly shrug at the residents who had witnessed this little conversation—as if to say, 'show's over, folks!' The last thing Essie needed was for the Happy Haven Director to get her dander up about her activities and start investigating. If Violet came by Essie's apartment unannounced and demanded to come inside, she would find baby Antonio and Essie's goose would be cooked. Worse, Violet would surely turn the baby over to social services and his mother—if she was still alive—might never get him back. Everything was a mess. Could things get any worse?

Essie headed out of the dining hall. She hadn't spoken to Santos, but she knew he knew where to find her if he needed her. She rolled into the lobby. The line at the front desk had diminished and Phyllis was now speaking to one of the staff nurses. As Essie rolled by she heard their conversation.

"Mildred McKensie, last night," said the young nurse, dressed in her colorful animal print jumpsuit, leaning over the desk, as she and Phyllis glanced together at a list. "Then, of course, Adele Anderson, you remember. This morning right here in the lobby." The nurse pointed to a name on the list.

"Yes," replied Phyllis, making a mark on the list with a pencil.

"Then we just had four more within the last hour," said the nurse and rattled off the names of several more residents. The doctor confirmed it."

"Blood tests?" asked Phyllis.

"Running them now. The doctor expects them to be positive for Mildred," replied. "And Adele. We expect the same for these other four." The two women looked at each other.

"Pretty violent symptoms," said the nurse. "Looks like a very contagious stomach virus."

Essie heard the last phrase "stomach virus" as she was rounding the decorated tree and heading back down her hallway. This was a really frightening development. A contagious disease of any sort in an assisted living facility could be dangerous. Even though she'd had her annual flu shot, she knew there were always strains of viruses that managed to make it through that barrier and cause havoc at many places such as Happy Haven where groups of people lived together. And, of course, there was the baby. Infants were particularly susceptible to contagious diseases. And she and her friends were keeping him here in a hothouse of germs. What were they thinking?

She rolled quickly down her hallway and into her apartment. Her three friends were feeding the baby with the glove bottle. Essie came in quickly and closed the door. She heaved a deep sigh and then told them the news.

"There's a bug going around," she announced dramatically, "and Violet thinks we're holding wild parties!"

Chapter Fifteen

"If your baby is 'beautiful and perfect, never cries or fusses, sleeps on schedule and burps on demand, an angel all the time,' you're the grandma."
–Theresa Bloomingdale

"Essie, your phone's been ringing off the hook!" said Marjorie as Essie stormed into her living room. "What do you mean bug?"

"And what wild parties?" asked Opal, looking up from the sofa, baby Antonio cuddled warmly in her lap.

Essie moved to her favorite chair and flung herself down with a sigh. "Violet accosted me in the lunchroom. Seems Clara Monroe complained about the noise we've been making!" Her three friends looked concerned.

"What noise?" cried Marjorie with a loud gasp, then suddenly whispered, "What noise?"

"I think Clara's just jealous," replied Essie in a similarly soft voice. "She sees the four of us going and coming from here and feels left out. That's all I can think of. The baby just doesn't cry that much." Fay nodded to this last statement and patted Antonio where he was quietly slurping his dinner in Opal's arms.

"Should we ask her to join us?" asked Opal as she squeezed the glove bottle gently to help baby Antonio secure the last few drops of substitute formula. Antonio playfully pushed the bottle away and stretched. "Here, Fay, why don't you put him on Essie's bed and see if he'll fall asleep?"

Fay carefully took the little boy in her arms and expertly drove her automated vehicle silently into Essie's bedroom.

"Heaven's to Hermione!" exclaimed Essie in response to Opal's suggestion. "Don't you think we have enough of us involved as it is?"

"I, for one, don't want to involve Clara," said Marjorie, conspiratorially. "She's always turning her nose up at me. I've spoken politely to her but she acts like she's better than everyone else." She shifted her shoulders back and forth and stuck out her lip in a pout. Essie often thought that Marjorie was very much like the grade schoolers she used to teach.

"I don't know about that," argued Essie, "or if she just doesn't know how to go about making friends . . ."

"Certainly not by complaining about her neighbors!" declared Opal, slapping her arm decisively on the end of Essie's flowered sofa. Opal was all about mature and responsible behavior. She had had to mollify many an irate employee and customer in her many years as an administrative assistant and she had been very good at her job.

"And what did you say about a bug?" asked Marjorie, all excited..

"What did you say about my telephone?" countered Essie. "You didn't answer it, did you?"

"Of course not!" exclaimed Opal with a huff. "That would take a lot of explaining, now wouldn't it? And, besides, it wouldn't be proper."

"It depends on who was calling," suggested Marjorie. "Most of the calls I get are from people conducting surveys or trying to get me to buy a timeshare vacation home in Bermuda. If it was one of those people, I don't think they'd know or care who answered the phone."

"But what if it was Essie's doctor? Or . . . worse . . . what if it was Violet?" asked Opal. "If she's suspicious of us, she just might call to check up on Essie."

"Or worse, she just might drop by," added Essie. "That's what really scares me. She is the Director. She has a master key. She can walk in any apartment at Happy Haven whenever she wants."

"Oh, Essie," said Marjorie, "she can't just go around barging into our apartments without a really good reason." She flopped her head of curls back and forth in a child-like manner.

"And now she has a good reason," replied Essie. "Clara has given her one."

"She would need more reason than one resident complaining about a noisy neighbor to just enter an apartment unannounced," said Opal, logically. "I think that's unlikely, Essie. But I do agree that Violet is probably going to be watching you . . . and us . . . more closely. We need to be much more careful what we do. We need to be especially quiet and we need to try to keep Antonio as quiet as possible."

"But Opal," said Marjorie, "he's a baby! Babies cry!"

"True," agreed Essie, "but there's four of us. We all need to work together to anticipate his needs before he has the need to cry."

"Good luck!" said Opal, ever the pragmatist.

As the three women continued to argue, Fay returned to the living room, pushing the bedroom door shut behind her. She put her finger to her plump little lips to indicate that the infant was sleeping. The women all put their fingers to their lips to indicate that they got Fay's message.

Marjorie whispered, "Essie, what did you say about bugs? Something about the exterminator?"

"No," whispered Essie in response, "a flu bug. I overheard one of the nurses talking to Phyllis at the front desk. Several residents have caught a nasty bug, it appears. Remember Adele Anderson this morning?"

"So, it wasn't food poisoning?" asked Marjorie.

"They don't know," replied Essie. "They're running lab tests. It looks like the same strain as the lady who got sick in the dining hall this morning. This has me more worried than anything. I've had my flu shot... "

"Me too!" declared Opal.

"And me!" added Marjorie. Fay nodded to their statements and pointed to herself, as she drove her wheelchair into the circle.

"Yes," said Essie, "but Antonio hasn't! And he's more susceptible than anyone! He's a newborn. He hasn't been seen by a doctor. Who knows what underlying physical ailments he might have that might compromise his immune system . . ."

"Essie," argued Marjorie, "Antonio seems very healthy. His skin isn't sallow. He's nice and plump and he's very responsive."

"Says Dr. Marjorie?" responded Essie. "You taught second grade, Marjorie. You aren't a pediatrician. If one of us comes down with this virus, Antonio will be in great jeopardy!" The four women sat frozen, staring at each other contemplating the seriousness of this most recent development.

"As I see it," said Opal finally, laying out their options, "it's a toss up. Maybe Antonio would be safer from a contagion standpoint if the four of us were not involved, but from a workload standpoint, Essie, it . . . takes a village . . . or so they say, to raise a child. At least, at Happy Haven, it takes four senior citizens to care for one newborn. Face it; we can barely take care of ourselves!"

"I resent that, Opal!" exclaimed Essie. "I get along quite well."

"As long as you have your aide to dress you in the morning and get you into your pajamas at night," added Marjorie, poking Essie playfully.

"The same as you!" retorted Essie. The escalating argument was cut off when Essie's telephone rang.

"Oh, no!" cried Essie. "We've been too loud. That's probably Violet calling to inform us that Clara is complaining again."

"It's better that she call to complain," noted Opal wisely, "than she show up at your front door!"

"That's right!" said Marjorie. The phone rang a second time. Marjorie carefully lifted the receiver from the phone, holding it as if it were a rattlesnake, and handed it to Essie.

"Hello," said Essie tentatively but pleasantly into the mouthpiece. "Oh, Claudia," Essie said with a relieved sigh. She continued to listen and nod, her face taking on a look of greater and greater despair. "Yes, Claudia, I'm thrilled that Kurt arrived early. Uh hum. The program's at four. " Essie rolled her eyes for the benefit of her three friends. "Truly, Claudia, I wish we didn't have to do this today." She gave a pitiful sigh into the receiver. Fay, Opal, and Marjorie nodded encouragingly to Essie and motioned her efforts with gestures. "Why not? Because . . . because . . . there's some sort of bug going around." She listened to her daughter's reaction. "Oh, no, dear, I'm fine, but, you know, some of the residents are pretty sick and . . ."

"Tell her you think you should stay in your room," suggested Opal.

"Tell her you don't want them to be around a lot of sick people," added Marjorie. Essie attempted to listen to her two friends and to her daughter on the telephone at the same time.

"Yes, dear," said Essie into the telephone, "yes, I know I have to eat. Of course, I want to see Kurt. It will be lovely to have you three children take me out, I'm sure." Essie cringed and ran her palm over her forehead. Fay, Opal, and Marjorie looked back and forth from one to the other.

"Don't worry, Essie!" whispered Marjorie. "If your children insist on coming over and taking you out to dinner, the three of us can watch Antonio in one of our rooms until you return." Opal and Fay nodded their heads to Marjorie's promise.

"Yes, dear," said Essie into the phone. "I guess I'll go with you. Yes, you'll be here a little before four. In time for the caroling program. Yes, dear. It does sound lovely! Okay. See you then!" Essie gently placed the receiver back in the telephone cradle. Her shoulders sagged noticeably as she looked from one friend to another. "Are you sure you three can handle this?"

"Haven't we been doing a fairly good job so far?" queried Opal with a shoulder point to the bedroom.

"Oh, I didn't mean to imply that you all aren't competent," said Essie quickly.

"Then, don't, Essie," said Marjorie. "Just go out with your family and let the three of us take care of Antonio. When you get back, we'll bring him back down."

"Fine," agreed Essie. "I guess if we're going to transfer Antonio from one location to another, we should make arrangements now."

"Yes," said Opal, sitting upright on the sofa and gesturing for their attention, as if she were conducting a meeting. "What I suggest is that the three of us return here around three or three thirty to pick up the baby and his belongings. That should give you time enough to get ready for your children before they get here at four. Then when you get back from dinner, just call me . . ."

"Why doesn't she call me, Opal?" interjected Marjorie. "We can keep Antonio in my apartment."

"It doesn't matter," said Opal. "All of our apartments are virtually the same."

"Why not Fay's apartment?" offered Essie, in an attempt to squelch the budding argument. "Does it matter? Actually, come to think of it, I suggest you all go to Marjorie's place because it's closest to mine . . . on the same floor. You'll be less likely to run into anyone . . . especially Violet or Clara . . . transferring the baby from here to there and back again."

"She's right," agreed Opal, deferring to logic. "Marjorie's apartment it is then. Fay and I will meet you there, Marjorie, and then we can all head over here to pick up the baby."

"Great!" said Essie. "Now, as Antonio is sound asleep, I suggest we all adjourn to our own places and rest up. I, for one, know that I'll need to relax before things get really hectic later this afternoon."

"We'll get going, Essie," agreed Opal. "We've put plenty of cans of substitute formula in case you need it."

"And a stack of baby diapers that Fay made out of those Reliables are piled up in the cupboard over your toilet," added Marjorie.

"Super Cooper!" exclaimed Essie. "It seems I'm a prepared babysitter!"

"Now all you need is for your boyfriend Hubert Darby to come over for a make-out session on the couch!" suggested Marjorie with a sassy smile.

"Marjorie!" gasped Opal.

"Let's concentrate on the 'baby' in our babysitting," said Essie, shaking her head.

The three friends rolled their respective vehicles to Essie's front door and quietly departed. Essie peeked around outside of her door to the left where Clara Monroe's apartment door was . . . about ten feet down the hallway. She could see the giant silver wreath on Clara's door. For someone with such a public display of Christmas spirit, Essie reasoned, Clara was not the most generous of souls. Was she just jealous? Or lonely? Why would she complain about Essie's behavior? Essie was quite sure that she and Marjorie, Opal, and Fay had not made any excessive noise in taking care of baby Antonio. If Clara had noticed the baby crying, why wouldn't she just mention that? It seems that complaining that a resident had a baby in their apartment for any period of time other than a brief visit would be sufficient grounds for concern. But no, Clara had complained that Essie had visitors and that they were making too much noise. Did Clara feel she was being left out of some sort of wild hallway party? Essie didn't know. Her attempts to befriend Clara had not succeeded and she wasn't sure that she should make any additional efforts.

Essie rolled back into her living room and to her bedroom door. She carefully cracked the door a few inches so she could check inside to see if baby Antonio was still asleep. He was. Like a little angel. Whatever miserable beginning his little life had had, he was one sweet-natured and well behaved infant. Surely, he didn't deserve the wrath of Clara Monroe. Essie pulled the door closed and rolled back over to her lounger. She plopped down in the soft cushions and pulled up the foot rest. Within a few moments she was sound asleep.

Chapter Sixteen

"Babies have big heads and big eyes, and tiny little arms and legs. So did the aliens at Roswell! I rest my case."
—William Shatner

When she woke up, Essie felt refreshed. Her watch indicated that she had slept just a half hour but it felt like more. She glanced over at the gift package of peanut brittle from Hubert Darby that was resting on her end table. She could always re-gift it to someone in a Secret Santa drawing. Oh, no, she reasoned. Hubert would find out and that would hurt his feelings. I'll just give it to my grandchildren.

Her hand went to her pants' pocket where she retrieved the small blue wallet that Santos had found in Maria and Gerald's apartment. She again looked inside. The only item there was a green card. The name on the card said Maria Compton. Hmm, thought Essie. Apparently one branch of the government considered Maria to be Gerald Compton's wife. Just how legal was their marriage? Just how legal was Maria? Or baby Antonio? Essie knew nothing of immigration law. She examined the small thin wallet, looking for hidden compartments. Other than some small change and a few dollar bills, the wallet contained nothing else.

Essie pushed herself out of her lounger, leaning against her walker. Why would just a little nap so adversely affect my knees? She got up and moved into her bathroom for a quick refresher. She pulled open the cupboard above her sink where her friends had hidden the makeshift diapers for Antonio. The little pink packages were lined up neatly. There were about thirty or forty of them. Enough to last several days, Essie reasoned. She glanced in her mirror. Oh my, she said to herself. My hair looks like it's been combed with an eggbeater! She remembered that when she had been a young mother, her appearance was the least of her concerns too. Her first child, Pru, had kept her awake at night a lot and her husband had not done much to assist her. Of course, in those days, it was the woman's duty to care for the children. Men did not get up at night to attend to cranky babies. Nowadays, there was more equality, or so she had heard. Of course, Gerald Compton evidently wasn't aware of any of this. He apparently had been living in the dark ages as far as how a modern father should behave. Essie fluffed up her sparkling silver curls with her fingertips and tweaked her cheeks to give them a healthy glow. Then she headed back to her living room to see what else she could do to track down Antonio's mother before the little boy awoke from his nap.

She quickly tracked down the telephone number of the newspaper she had called earlier. This time, she was rewarded when the reporter who had written the article on Gerald Compton's fatal automobile crash, Bernice McVickers, answered her telephone extension.

"Ms. McVickers?" asked Essie.

"You got me," replied the woman succinctly.

"I spoke with your colleague Mr. Watts earlier," said Essie. "He filled me in on the story you wrote about that fatal car crash on the corner of Farris and Orchard, but he suggested I talk to you about the specifics . . ." She tried to sound authoritative.

"And you are?" asked McVickers.

"Uh . . . " stammered Essie. "I . . . uh . . . live in the neighborhood where the crash occurred . . ."

"You do?" interjected the reporter. "Did you know this guy? The victim?"

"You mean Gerald Compton?" asked Essie.

"Yeah," replied the woman, "the whole accident was strange . . ."

"Strange?" probed Essie.

"Yeah," continued McVickers. "The guy was flying down a residential street. Completely oblivious of this other car in the intersection, legally, I might add. The police think . . . you know . . . maybe suicidal? Anyway, did you know him?"

"Um . . . not personally," replied Essie, "but I did know of him."

"Yeah," replied the reporter, now with curiosity, "I questioned a number of neighbors around the intersection. Don't remember you. It was just a block from his home."

"Yes," said Essie, now getting excited that the conversation was turning to an aspect that might prove valuable to her. "I had heard that the man's wife wasn't questioned . . ."

"Wife?" cried the voice at the news office, "Hey! What wife? The Compton guy wasn't married. He was driving his father's car. As far as we were able to determine, he lived alone."

"The father told the police that?" asked Essie.

"That's my understanding," said McVickers. "The father was the only surviving relative."

"My understanding was that Mr. Compton had a wife and a child," offered Essie.

"What? If that's true," said the woman suspiciously, "the dead guy's father was lying . . . and why would he lie about something like that?"

"Yes," replied Essie. "Why would he lie?"

"The police spoke with Compton's landlord. He said Compton lived alone."

"Really?" asked Essie, puzzled.

"So, what's this wife's name? Where is she?" continued the reporter, "And how would you know this? Hey, what did you say your name was?"

"I didn't," replied Essie, fearing she'd probably said too much and wondering now if revealing the existence of Maria and her baby as Gerald Compton's wife and child had been the best thing to do. Biting her lip, she gently placed the receiver back on the telephone base.

This entire debacle was becoming stranger and stranger. Just what was the relationship between Gerald and Maria Compton? Were they married? Legally? If not, what was going on? If so, why was Gerald keeping his relationship with Maria a secret? From his father? His employer? His landlord? Evidently everyone? It was looking more and more as if Maria had no legal claim to American citizenship. Essie had no idea what lay in store for little Antonio given the unusual circumstances surrounding his parents. Could things get any worse?

At that moment, the PA system crackled. Oh no, more announcements. Luckily, the announcements had not been blasting away when she was talking to the newspaper reporter. She recognized Phyllis's voice on the intercom.

"Residents!" said Phyllis in a serious voice, "I have an important announcement that will affect all of you. It appears that a rather fast-moving and serious stomach virus may have hit Happy Haven. Just within the last few hours, we've had eight residents become quite ill. Three have been hospitalized. Our staff doctor and our nurses have been discussing just how to deal with this potentially very serious virus. We have decided that as a precautionary measure we're going to quarantine the entire facility until further notice. This means that no resident is to leave his or her apartment for any reason other than a scheduled outside appointment such as a doctor's visit. Staff members will bring you your meals and we will have additional nurses' aides on duty to assist if any of you need help. Please call the front desk if you have any concerns or need anything. Otherwise, do not leave your apartment. The dining hall and the family room and all other areas in Happy Haven where residents might congregate are now officially off limits. Oh, and we are so sorry that we will have to cancel the Christmas carol program that was scheduled today for four o'clock. We will be bringing you updates on the status of our quarantine from time to time. Please watch for bulletins put under your doors as well."

Essie sat in her chair, flabbergasted. Of course, she was grateful that Happy Haven was taking precautions to prevent the spread of disease. Of course, she did not want to catch any stomach virus that might be making the rounds of her fellow residents. She had already seen several of them succumb to it–thankfully–from a distance. But, what was she going to do about Antonio? A quarantine meant that her friends would not be allowed to come to her room. Opal and Marjorie and Fay would all have to remain in their own apartments.

The telephone rang . . . loudly. Essie answered it, annoyed that anyone would break into her attempts to figure out this most recent dilemma.

"Essie," exclaimed Opal into the receiver, "did you hear the announcement?"

"No, Opal!" replied Essie, "I happen to be the only person at Happy Haven who didn't hear that we are all under a quarantine!"

"What about Antonio?" demanded Opal.

"What about him?" retorted Essie. "I'll have to watch him myself!"

"What about your children?" continued Opal.

"I'm trying to figure that out," replied Essie. "But I can't do that when I'm talking to you!" She hung up. If Opal was offended, she was sorry, but right now she had to figure out what to do when her three children arrived to take her out for dinner. Maybe they wouldn't let her go! That's a thought! she reasoned. She called the front desk.

"Phyllis," she began.

"Yes?" replied Phyllis, sounding harried.

"Phyllis, this is Essie Cobb," said Essie, "in B114."

"Yes, dear," answered Phyllis, "are you sick?"

"Oh, no!" replied Essie, "I feel just fine. I was wondering if I'm allowed to go out to dinner tonight. My children want to take me out. Of course, if you say I can't go, I don't mind telling them . . . ."

"Oh, no, Essie!" said Phyllis. "The quarantine only applies to interacting with other residents! We have no problem with you going out with your children . . . as long as you're well!"

"Hmm," answered Essie, "what are the symptoms of this virus"

"It comes on very suddenly," said Phyllis, "vomiting, fever, chills, diarrhea . . ."

"Sounds terrible," replied Essie, feeling ill just hearing Phyllis describe it. "I guess I don't have it."

"That's good, Essie," said Phyllis. "You just stay in your room! But if you want to go out to dinner with your family! That's fine But I'd be sure to let them know about the quarantine."

Essie mumbled her thanks to Phyllis who quickly hung up. It was obvious that Phyllis was going to be very busy at the front desk answering questions from residents who were now stuck in their rooms. She had almost hoped that Happy Haven would extend the quarantine to residents leaving the building but no such luck. Here she was now, alone in her apartment with a newborn baby. Her three children would be here in just hours to take her out to dinner. She obviously couldn't go with them and leave the baby all alone. She couldn't have any of her three friends come down and stay here or take the baby with them. The staff would be watching the hallways and the lobby to make certain that residents remained in their rooms. What could she do? If she told her children the truth, they would insist she give Antonio to the authorities. She couldn't leave Antonio alone while she went out with her family. If he cried while she was gone, she'd be found out And, of course, she'd never leave him alone.

Oh, well, she mused, at least I have a few hours to try to figure out what to do. Maybe Maria would pop up at her door and take her baby back! Like, duh, as her grandson Nathan often said. The phone rang again.

"Essie," cried Marjorie, "you're there!"

"And where else would I be, Marjorie?" asked Essie, annoyed that her friend had the gall to think she'd be running around the halls while a quarantine was in effect.

"Is Antonio okay?"

"Yes," replied Essie. "He's still asleep, despite the fact that my phone has been ringing off the hook and the public address system has been droning on and on . . ."

"What are we going to do, Essie?" asked Marjorie.

"What do you mean 'we,' Marjorie?" demanded Essie. "The three of you are out of this! Antonio is in my bedroom! He's my problem now . . . as long as this quarantine is in place!"

"But your children?" cried Marjorie into the phone, obviously flustered.

"I'm sorry, Marjorie," said Essie, calmly. "That was unfair of me. It's not your fault . . . or Opal's or Fay's . . . that some ghastly virus is probably right now spreading all over our home. I'm just at my wits' end as to what to do. I've tried to convince my children not to come, but no luck."

"I'm sorry, Essie," said Marjorie. "I guess we're going to have to tell Violet."

Essie envisioned Violet with a baby . . . with sweet little Antonio. The stern, unfeeling director of Happy Haven, glaring down at a small infant through her long, carefully curled eyelashes was an image Essie couldn't bring herself to accept. There had to be a better way. There had to be a way to find Antonio's mother. If

Maria was dead, her body had not been found . . . that was the only thing to which Essie now clung.

"No," said Essie to Marjorie. "I'm not giving up." She continued to clutch the telephone receiver making an unseen connection with her friend through the telephone line. "Marjorie," she said finally, "what about Fay?"

"Fay?" repeated Marjorie, "What about her?"

"She can't or won't speak, you know," noted Essie. "What if she gets sick in her room? How will she contact the front desk?"

"I don't know," responded Marjorie in a sad little voice. "I never thought about that."

"I wonder if the staff ever thought about it either," said Essie. "I'm sure Fay is not the only resident who can't contact the front desk."

"I tell you what, Essie," said Marjorie, "I'm going to call the front desk myself and suggest a staff member go check on Fay."

"That's a wonderful idea, Marjorie," said Essie. "In the mean time, I'm going to try to find Antonio's mother. Maybe I can locate her before my children show up."

The phones clicked at almost the same time. Essie thought how much in tune she was with her friends and how much she'd miss their help in taking care of Antonio.

Chapter Seventeen
"For soothing out our infant worries with a softly spoken song."
–Bill Ronan

Essie sat and pondered the information she had about Maria Valdez Compton and her husband Gerald. She realized that her most urgent problem was to find a way to deal with baby Antonio when her children came to take her out. She lifted her telephone receiver and dialed Claudia's number.

"Yes?" answered her youngest daughter, breathlessly. Claudia always sounded as if she was in the middle of another activity.

"Claudia," began Essie, "I have some bad news."

"Oh no!" replied her daughter, now concerned. "What's wrong?"

"Happy Haven is under quarantine," replied Essie with solemnity. She hoped this news might convince her children to forego their efforts to take her out to dinner.

"What?" cried Claudia. "Why?"

"They think it's a stomach virus going around," replied Essie.

"Are you sick, Mom?" asked Claudia.

"No! No, dear!" said Essie, now upset that she had worried her daughter unnecessarily. "I'm fine, really I am. It just seems to have hit really hard and many residents have become quite sick, quite suddenly."

"So they're quarantining the place?" asked Claudia. "What does that mean exactly?"

"It means we all have to stay in our rooms. We can't go to the family room or lobby or anywhere else in the building."

"What about the dining hall?" asked Claudia.

"Definitely not there," replied Essie, "I saw a lady get sick there myself. Terrible."

"How do they expect everyone to eat?" asked Claudia, ever practical.

"Oh, they'll bring us our meals," said Essie. "But they've cancelled the caroling program for this afternoon."

"Oh, no!" said Claudia. "But, of course. They wouldn't want to expose all those young children to the virus." Essie felt immediately guilty when Claudia started talking about children becoming ill. All she could think about was the little baby asleep on her bed who was now smack dab in the middle of a major germ zone.

"So no one is allowed to leave?" asked Claudia.

"We can leave the building," replied Essie, "but you and Kurt and Prudence might not really want to come over here. I mean, there's this bug going around. You three surely don't want to expose yourselves to it."

"Oh, for heaven's sake, Mom," exclaimed Claudia, "we're tough! Kurt wants to see you! He drove all the way down to Reardon. And besides, you'll probably appreciate getting out. You must be bored to tears just sitting there in your apartment all day long with nothing to do!" Essie cringed when her daughter said this last sentence. Bored was the last thing she was.

"Oh, no, Claudia," she said, "I'm just fine. It's actually quite pleasant to be able to relax and just sit here..."

"Don't be silly," interjected Claudia, "we're not going to let you just stay there all alone and eat supper in your room! We're coming to get you and take you out to a nice restaurant! How about that little Italian one we went to the last time Kurt was in town? You said you loved their ravioli!"

"Yes, it was very nice," responded Essie.

"Then, it's settled," replied Claudia. "Since there's not going to be any concert, we'll come around five to get you. How about that? I know you like to eat early."

"Yes, dear," said Essie. "Early. Five." They said their good-byes and hung up. Essie tapped her fingers on the arms of her lounger. She looked at her watch. It was a little after two in the afternoon. It was not going to be possible to change Claudia's mind. Her children would be there at five to take her to dinner. Somehow, she'd have to figure out what to do about Antonio between now and then.

A sharp knock sounded at her door. She pushed down her footrest on her lounge chair and rose.

Rolling her walker to the door, she called out, "Who's there?"

"It's Barbara, the staff nurse, Miss Essie," said a muffled voice. Essie cracked the door.

"Yes?" she replied to the woman standing at her door wearing a face mask.

"Miss Essie," began the nurse, "we're going around to all the residents to check vitals and symptoms. We just want to be very cautious because of this virus." The nurse's eyes twinkled merrily behind the green paper mask.

"Oh, yes," said Essie, "but I'm fine. I don't have any symptoms." She worried that the baby would awaken from his nap at any moment and cry out. If this nurse heard him, she would be more than curious.

"May I come in, please? It will just take a minute," said the nurse, now actually starting to push her way into Essie's apartment.

"I . . . guess so," replied Essie, backing up with her walker into her living room. The nurse closed the door behind her and motioned for Essie to sit. Then, she quickly removed a thermometer from a kit hanging from her shoulder and shoved it into Essie's mouth.

"Ixmlbhhmm," mumbled Essie, holding the thermometer tightly in her lips. The nurse expertly wrapped a blood pressure cuff around Essie's arm and pumped it up. Then she slowly allowed the air to release. She wrapped the cuff and the long tube extending from it up and put it back in her shoulder bag.

"Good, 123 over 74," said the nurse. She grabbed the thermometer from Essie's mouth and read it. "98.6. Excellent. How are you feeling?"

"I'm fine," replied Essie, starting to stand up and aim the nurse back to her front door. "If I feel sick, I'll let you know."

"Good," said Barbara. "You're eating okay? You're not feeling nauseous?"

"No," replied Essie, "I'm just fine! My appetite is just fine too!" She smiled warmly at the nurse and gently placed a hand on the woman's back as she edged her to the door.

"Wonderful!" Nurse Barbara said, turning back to her. "Let's just hope you stay that way!" She tucked the lid of her medical kit closed and headed out of Essie's apartment.

"Yes, let's!" responded Essie, closing the door abruptly in the nurse's face. She hoped that the nurse did not feel offended because Essie did appreciate the concern that Happy Haven was showing the residents in light of this recent outbreak. However, the last thing Essie needed was for anyone else to become aware of baby Antonio in her apartment.

As soon as Essie had closed the door, she rolled her walker back inside and took a quick peek into her bedroom. Antonio was starting to stir. She could see his chubby legs sticking up in the air. Soon he would want something to drink. Although she wanted to do more investigating into the whereabouts of his mother, Essie realized that her first duty now was to take care of Antonio. She rolled to her kitchen and opened her refrigerator door and pulled out one of the cans of protein drink that Opal had left her. Quickly she prepared the empty but clean glove bottle that Opal had left in the refrigerator. She let it run under the hot water then filled it with the formula. Then she re-closed the top with the rubber band and ran the entire contraption under the hot water until the tiny stream from the needle hole in the little finger of the glove ran at room temperature. Then, she set the device on her walker seat and headed into her bedroom where baby Antonio was now awake. She made herself comfortable on her bed beside the infant and lifted him into her arms. The baby quickly began gyrating, his signal–she assumed–that he was hungry. Essie grabbed the glove bottle and slid the finger nipple into Antonio's small mouth. Instantly, the infant calmed and began sucking contentedly.

Essie leaned back on the headboard of her bed and stared down at the baby's sweet face. The gash on his cheek did not seem as red and ugly as it had last night. As he drank his meal, Essie softly sang to him a song that she remembered singing to her own children many years ago:

> I see the moon
> The moon sees me
> God bless the moon
> and God bless me
>
> I see the stars
> The stars see me

God bless the stars
and God bless me

I see the world.
The world sees me.
God bless the world,
And God bless me.

I know an angel
Watches over me.
God bless the angels,
And God bless me."

Maybe, Essie hoped, some of these blessings would actually come true for baby Antonio.

Chapter Eighteen
"Babies are such a nice way to start people."
–Don Herrold

After Antonio downed the contents of his makeshift bottle and then promptly filled his tiny pink makeshift diapers, Essie quickly changed him and rocked him gently in her arms until he fell asleep. She placed the tiny infant on the center of her bed and rolled herself back out into her living room. She was exhausted. Glancing at her wristwatch, she realized that it was only two-thirty. Opening her telephone directory, she looked up the home number for Harold Compton, father of the late Gerald Compton. Perhaps he would be at home grieving for his son and she would be able to ask him a few questions. A man's voice responded after three or four rings.

"Yeah?" said the gruff voice.

"Mr. Compton?" asked Essie.

"Yeah," he replied. "Who's this?"

"Uh . . . you don't know me, but I heard about your son and I just wanted to offer my sympathy . . ." she answered cautiously.

"Yeah?" he yelled back, "what good is that?"

"I know, sir, that it's small compensation for the loss of a child . . . " she stammered.

"It was his own damn fault!" countered Harold Compton. "The kid was a stupid jerk! Always goin' off half cocked! A real hot head. He was an accident waiting to happen, lady! So don't waste your sympathy on him!"

"Oh, dear," she replied, flustered. "But what about his wife?"

"Oh, shit!" he swore. "Not you too! Who are you? Some bleeding heart do-gooder from immigration? That woman was using him! I told him over and over! She just wanted a green card and the minute she got legal, she'd dump him! I doubt that their 'marriage,' as you say, was even legal."

"But, sir, Mr. Compton," pleaded Essie, "what about the baby?"

"What baby?" he screamed into the receiver.

"I . . . I understand that Maria . . . his wife . . . just had a baby several days ago," she said, tentatively.

"Naw," replied Compton, "I saw that woman a few weeks ago. She wasn't pregnant."

"She wasn't?" asked Essie incredulously. Could it be possible that baby Antonio wasn't Maria Compton's child? Gerald Compton's child? "Did you speak to her?"

"Hell, no!" he said. "She came into the company looking for Gerald once. I told her to get lost. I told her to quit bothering my son and trying to scam him!"

"But she lived with Gerald," replied Essie. "Do you know where she might be now?"

"Look, lady, I don't know who you are or why you're so damned interested in my son's business. But he's dead so none of this really matters any more! I don't care where that bitch was living or where she is now. Gerald was no saint, but just because he goes through some hokey ceremony with some local when he's on vacation in Tijuana doesn't mean he's officially hitched to her . . . at least not here in the ol' US of A! All I know is that if that stupid whore hadn't latched onto my son, he'd be alive now!" With that, Harold Compton slammed the receiver down and Essie cringed as the silence at the other end of the line reverberated.

Obviously, the marriage–legal or otherwise–between Gerald and Maria was not accepted as such by Gerald's father. Harold Compton also wasn't aware or didn't want to admit that he was aware that his daughter-in-law had been pregnant and that he now had a grandson. Poor Antonio, thought Essie. If only Harold Compton had accepted Maria and embraced her as a member of the family, little Antonio would now have a place to call home. But, no way was Essie going to turn the infant over to this monster who would probably just hand him over to Immigration–if that. No, said Essie to herself, I'm going to redouble my efforts to find your mother, Antonio.

She picked up Maria's wallet from her end table and examined the green card inside. The small rectangular card was laminated. On the front of the green card (and, yes, it truly was printed in green ink), at the top, read "United States of America Permanent Resident." It featured a photograph of Maria Valdez Compton. Essie stared at the photo–Antonio's mother. She was a sweet-looking young woman with long, straight black hair, pulled back over her ears. Maria stared into the camera looking forlorn and unsmiling. Other information on the card indicated her country of birth: Mexico and her birthdate: January 7, 1991. It also listed a date when Maria became a resident, which Essie noted was over a year ago, and a date when her card would expire. As Essie turned the card over in her hands, she realized that the card exhibited other sophisticated features such as bar codes and imprinted holographs. It appeared that the backside of Maria's green card was a high-tech treasure trove. She again opened the small blue wallet and replaced the green card inside. As she held the tiny purse in her hands, it dawned on her that the green card was the single most important of Maria's personal possessions and that she would have guarded it carefully. She never would have willingly deserted it–any more than she would have deserted her baby.

Would Maria contact an Immigration office to replace her card? Essie believed that she would–if she were able. The fact that she had not yet returned to retrieve Antonio suggested to Essie that something very bad had happened to Maria Valdez Compton. She had not been in the car with her husband when he was killed–nor in the other car involved in the accident. Few people at Rose Brothers' Construction were aware of her or of Gerald's marriage to her—if such marriage truly existed. Gerald's father, Harold Compton, was aware of Maria, but blamed her for Gerald's accident, so it was unlikely that he was concerned about her welfare or whereabouts. He, Harold Compton, also did not appear to be aware that Maria had been pregnant or had given birth. The last anyone apparently saw Maria seemed to be last night, when she dropped Antonio off with Santos. From Santos's exploration of the Compton's apartment, it appeared that Maria must have returned home to pack after leaving Antonio with Santos, maybe planning to leave her husband. Possibly, Essie reasoned, Gerald returned to the apartment and found his wife packing. He may have become enraged and a fight ensued. During the fight, thought Essie, Maria managed to escape, but was not able to grab her wallet. Gerald followed her—with Maria on foot and Gerald in his car. From that point on, Essie continued to speculate what might have happened. Assuming both Gerald and Maria were very upset at this time, neither of them would have been thinking clearly. Obviously, Gerald's anger and lack of clear thinking was what probably led to his fatal car crash—given his high speed in a residential neighborhood. If Maria was running from Gerald, maybe she saw the crash. Maybe she didn't. Maybe she panicked and in her attempt to elude her husband, fell and was injured. Assuming she was on foot, the woman could be anywhere near her apartment. Essie knew the area where the Comptons lived and there were many wooded spots around it. If Maria had hurt herself or fallen in any of these locations, she could be lying on the ground–injured or even dead. Quite possibly, she could be out in the open and might not be discovered until spring. The weather was so bad, it would be unlikely that anyone would be out walking in the woods if they didn't have to be. Obviously, Essie could not go out in the snow to look for Maria in the woods. But Santos might be able to when he got off from his shift. She decided to ask him to check the wooded areas near Maria and Gerald's apartment when he had a chance. She lifted her receiver and called the main desk.

"Hello, Phyllis," she said when the familiar voice answered. "Can you give me the extension for the kitchen?"

"Do you need something, Essie?" asked Phyllis.

"Um . . . yes," she replied. "I just need to ask a favor of one of the workers."

"A favor! Oh!" replied Phyllis, somewhat surprised. "Just a moment, Essie, and I'll connect you." The phone rang several times in Essie's ear and then a cheery voice responded.

"Kitchen!"

"May I please speak with Santos?" she asked politely.

"Hey, Santos!" she heard the voice call out. "You got a caller!" Shortly, she recognized the young waiter's voice on the other end.

"Hello?"

"Santos, it's Essie Cobb," she said surreptitiously. "I'm sorry to bother you while you're working . . ."

"Miss Essie!" he exclaimed, then whispered, "Is baby okay?"

"Yes! He's fine!" she said. "I was wondering, Santos, if you might have a few moments to check out some of the wooded areas near Maria and Gerald's apartment? I'm thinking that since we haven't heard from Maria and she wasn't in the car with her husband when he was killed last night, that maybe she was trying to run from him. She did leave her wallet, so she must have left in a hurry. Maybe she wasn't able to come back for Antonio because she fell and is injured."

"You mean, she fall in woods, Miss Essie?" he cried in a whisper, obviously shielding the phone from anyone overhearing the conversation. "That is very bad! Weather very bad today!"

"I know, Santos!" agreed Essie. "That's why it's so important that you take a look around their apartment. If Maria is lying wounded somewhere out there, she could be unable to contact anyone. She could be . . . dead, Santos. We need to know. There has to be a reason she hasn't returned for Antonio. It certainly isn't that she's afraid of Gerald anymore."

"Maybe Maria not know Gerald is dead," suggested Santos.

"True!" agreed Essie, "but if she's anywhere inside, she's probably seen the news coverage of Gerald's accident. It's been all over the news and it was pretty gruesome."

"Gruesome?" asked Santos.

"Yes, terrible! Horrific!" explained Essie.

"Oh, si. Gruesome!" repeated Santos. "Very good English word, Miss Essie."

"Santos, enough with the vocabulary lesson," said Essie. "Can you go check the wooded areas around Maria's apartment?"

"Si, Miss Essie!" he replied. "I take break now. I have fifteen minutes for humo de romper . . . how you say, smoke cigarette."

"You don't smoke, do you, Santos?" she cried.

"Oh, no, Miss Essie," he said, "but I do the break!"

"Wonderful!" she responded. "So, get going. You have a car?"

"Si!" he said, "I have very nice American sports car. It is 1994 Ford Escort."

"Good for you," she chuckled, as the young man's pride in his vehicle was evident. "And Santos, let me know what you find out–even if you don't find anything."

"Si, Miss Essie," he said. "I report to you right away. Now I go!" He hung up quietly and Essie replaced her telephone receiver with a relief. She both hoped and dreaded that Santos would find something, that something being Maria lying injured somewhere near her home unable to move or contact help. If he didn't find her, the circumstances of baby Antonio appeared more and more bleak. She got up from her lounge chair and rolled over to her bedroom door where she could check on her charge. The baby was sleeping soundly. There were no leg movements which Essie realized were the signs that Antonio was stirring and would soon want to be fed. She sighed. Was there anything else she could do from her apartment while she waited for Santos to look for Maria?

Chapter Nineteen
"A new baby is like the beginning of all things—wonder, hope, a dream of possibilities."
–Eda J. LeShan

Essie sat drumming her fingers on the arm of her chair. Her heart was racing and her mind was too. There must be something else I could do for the little infant asleep on my bed, she thought. She looked out her window on the far side of her living room. Snow was coming down faster than it had been earlier and building up noticeably on the branches of the evergreens in the courtyard outside of Essie's window. Poor Santos! How was he going to search for Maria in this weather? If Maria was lying on the ground somewhere—injured—he might not see her if she was covered in snow. Of course, reasoned Essie, people had been known to survive injuries for days until help arrived. It had now been almost a full day since Maria had disappeared. But, surely, the cold weather would make surviving outdoors less and less likely, wouldn't it? If Santos couldn't find some trace of Maria, they would have to report her disappearance to the authorities. And they'd have to report Antonio too.

Essie rubbed her temples. This was not the kind of pleasant retirement she had envisioned for herself when she had moved to Happy Haven six years ago.

Yes, she enjoyed the camaraderie of her fellow residents, but how she managed to get herself into these pickles, she just didn't understand. I'm ninety years old, she wanted to cry out to the world! She was not an investigative reporter or a bloodhound. She just wanted to be able to relax in her lounge chair with her feet up and work on her puzzles. That thought made her reach over to her end table where she kept a clipboard of some of the most recent puzzles that she was working on. There were crosswords, picture puzzles, and a variety of other brain teasers. Essie perused the top puzzle which remained unfinished and chewed on the pencil that was attached to the clipboard with a string. Quickly, she filled in one of the empty words.

"Of course!" she said to herself out loud. "Why didn't I figure that one out before? Maybe all this detecting is making me sharper." She chuckled aloud, but not so loud that she would awaken baby Antonio.

She glanced over at the gift box that Hubert Darby had given her. "Peanut brittle," she moaned quietly. "Why couldn't he give me chocolates?" She picked up the box casually and pulled off the red bow and ribbon and unwrapped the package. Inside, she found a beautiful blue velvet jewelry box. "This isn't a candy box," she mused, cautiously lifting the attached lid. Inside, nestled on a blue velvet bed lay a gleaming golden necklace. A small heart-shaped pendant shone at the end of a delicate chain.

"Mothers of Murgatroyd!" exclaimed Essie. "What's this?" She lifted the delicate necklace up from its bed so she could examine it. "What's going on?" Looking more carefully at the box, she found a label from the designer on the inside of the lid. It was a company name she recognized–a company that was known for producing expensive jewelry. "Maybe this is Hubert's mother's necklace. Maybe he isn't aware of its value. Why would he give it to me? Surely, he didn't purchase it for me." She spoke to herself in a whisper as she continued to ponder the present on her lap.

Finally, she closed the lid of the jewelry box and placed it on her end table along with the remnants of the wrapping paper. "I can't accept this from Hubert . . . or anyone," she said out loud to anyone who might be listening. "It wouldn't be appropriate . . . no matter what this necklace is worth. And I'm guessing it's worth quite a lot." She grabbed the box and rewrapped the present, attempting to place the tape back in its original position. When she had it reasonably rewrapped, she placed it back on her end table.

"I don't need this now, Hubert," she said aloud. "Why couldn't you have just given me peanut brittle like you said you did? That would only be a problem for my teeth!" She slapped her forehead with her palm and rocked back and forth in her chair. The only good thing in the present situation was that with the quarantine in effect, she wouldn't have to confront

Hubert immediately; she'd at least have some time to figure out how to return the necklace to him politely and explain to him how inappropriate it is for men to give women expensive jewelry when they are merely acquaintances. At least, she assumed it was expensive jewelry. Even if it was a very clever fake, it was still inappropriate.

The phone rang, shaking her from her contemplation.

"Essie," said Marjorie's voice, "how is Antonio? I'm sorry to pester you. I just miss him so much."

"He's fine, Marjorie," replied Essie, actually happy for the interruption. "Did you have someone check on Fay?"

"Yes, yes!" she said. "They promised they would! The staff is aware of Fay's problems, Essie. They know she can't or won't use her telephone, so they will be checking on her a lot until we are all allowed to leave our rooms. Now! How is my baby?"

"Your baby?" retorted Essie. "Since when is he yours?"

"Our baby, then," replied Marjorie. "Is he eating? Do you have enough formula?"

"Yes, Marjorie, and, yes," said Essie. "Nothing has changed in the last few hours since you last saw Antonio. He's asleep now, although I'm surprised he manages to stay asleep with all the commotion."

"What commotion?"

"Santos was here earlier," she reported, "and now he's out looking for Maria."

"Where?" asked Marjorie excitedly. "Did you get a lead on her?"

"No, Marjorie," replied Essie, "no lead, but the longer she remains missing, the more I worry that she's injured somewhere and unable to contact anyone . . . or worse yet . . . dead."

"Oh, Essie," exclaimed Marjorie, "I hope not! So where is Santos looking?"

"In the woods next to her home," said Essie. "I . . . we were thinking that maybe she and Gerald fought and she ran out to get away from him and he chased after her. Maybe that's when he got in that car accident. We know Maria couldn't drive and didn't have a car and we know she wasn't in the car with Gerald, so we are assuming she was on foot and probably couldn't get very far from her apartment."

"I hope he finds her," said Marjorie, sighing deeply.

"Me too," agreed Essie. "And that's not all of my problems!" she confided in a whisper.

"What else?" queried Marjorie.

"You'll never believe it!" Essie huffed into the receiver. "The peanut brittle that Hubert Darby gave me turns out to be a gold necklace!"

"What?"

"Yes, it's true. I just opened the present and instead of candy, there was a jewelry box from Kreigsted's!"

"Kreigsted's! Oh, Essie, they're expensive!" gushed Marjorie.

"I know!" replied Essie. "It's a blue velvet box. Inside is this beautiful gold pendant!"

"Is Hubert wealthy?" asked Marjorie. "He doesn't seem wealthy."

"What does a wealthy man seem like?" snickered Essie. She was amazed that Marjorie would hone in on the most unimportant aspect of her problem.

"I don't know," she replied, "I mean, he doesn't act like he has a lot of money."

"No, he doesn't," Essie agreed. "I'm thinking maybe it's his mother's or something. Maybe he doesn't even realize that it's worth something."

"What are you going to do, Essie?"

"I'm not going to keep it," she said, "that's for certain. I'll have to return it. Obviously, not now. But as soon as the quarantine is lifted."

"It's going to hurt Hubert's feelings, Essie," said Marjorie sadly. "He really has a crush on you."

"Marjorie," said Essie firmly, "I can't accept expensive presents from a man I barely know."

"I don't know why not," suggested Marjorie coyly, "I would. Hubert can give me expensive jewelry if he wants."

"Oodles of doodles, Marjorie!" exclaimed Essie. "Have you no scruples?"

"There's nothing wrong with accepting a gift from a man!"

"Peanut brittle, no! Expensive jewelry, yes!"

"Essie, you don't even know for sure that it's expensive."

"I'm pretty sure that it is," said Essie, now thinking about the necklace in the beautiful box that remained wrapped in its original green paper on her end table.

"You know who would know for sure?" offered Marjorie.

"Who?"

"Opal," replied Marjorie. "She rambles on often enough about that 'namesake' opal she wears around her neck. She thinks she's an expert on all things jewel-related. I'm going to call her and . . ."

Essie interrupted her. "Marjorie, I'm sorry I even mentioned Hubert's gift. This just isn't something I want to have to worry about now . . . or have you and Opal worry about. We have to think about Antonio . . . and his mother."

"What can we do for either of them now?" pleaded Marjorie.

"Nothing," said Essie eventually with a sigh.

"Then, let me talk to Opal about your necklace. I'm sure she'll know whether it's worth something and she might even have an idea about what you should do with it . . . and Hubert Darby."

"Oh, all right!" agreed Essie. The two women said their good-byes and Essie pulled herself out of her chair and rolled over to her bedroom door to see if her little charge was still sleeping. He was.

There was a soft knock on her door. Essie scooted quickly to the door and cracked it slightly. Santos stood in the hallway dressed in his winter jacket and hat. He was stomping snow off of his shoes and looking around cautiously from side to side.

"Miss Essie," he whispered. "Can I come in?"

"Yes, yes, of course," she replied, opening the door to allow the young man to enter. Santos moved inside quickly and went directly to Essie's bedroom door where he looked briefly in to see baby Antonio still sleeping.

"Not good news, Miss Essie," said Santos. "I find this." He abruptly removed a small rectangular-shaped white plastic nameplate from his pants' pocket. Essie took it from his freezing fingers and examined it as she leaned against the handles of her walker. It appeared to be a nametag that an employee might wear at work. On the back was a long pin where the tag attached to the employee's clothes. The pin was bent backwards and a small remnant of white cloth was attached to it. On the front side of the nametag were printed the words "Happy Haven" in bright blue cursive letters at the top, and in the middle typed on a strip of adhesive marking tape, the name 'Maria.'"

"Oh, no!" cried Essie. "This is Maria's?"

"Si, Miss Essie," said Santos. "Just like mine." He opened his heavy jacket and pointed at a similar nametag on his apron. "I find it in a ditch very close to Maria's apartment. Snow almost covers name tag. I look everywhere nearby, Miss Essie, but I do not find Maria."

"Maybe she fell there and lost her tag," suggested Essie, "and then got up."

"Then where is Maria?" asked Santos. "She does not come to work. She does not call Santos to get baby. Where is Maria?"

"I don't know, Santos," replied Essie, "but finding this nametag certainly indicates that Maria was there in the woods at one point. Maybe she fell, but then maybe she got up and was able to walk away. I think that's a good sign. It means she's ambulatory."

"I do not know this big English word, Miss Essie," said Santos.

"She was able to walk," replied Essie.

Oh, si! Like 'ambulance'," he said.

"Yes," agreed Essie. "Like ambulance. Maybe she was able to get to a hospital and get help. Or maybe someone helped her."

"So why she does not call Santos? Why she does not call about baby?"

"That is the big question, Santos," said Essie. "I think we're going to have to call the authorities about Antonio . . . ."

"No!" cried Santos, grabbing Essie's hands on her walker handlebars. "Please, Miss Essie! Please wait more time for Maria. I know Maria is very good mother. Maria does not . . . how you say . . . abandonará . . ."

"Yes," said Essie, "abandon. That's the word. But Santos, I'm afraid it's no longer a case of Maria abandoning Antonio. It's a case of Maria's safety too. The very fact that she hasn't returned for her baby suggests that something horrible may have happened to her..."

"But, Miss Essie," he pleaded, "Gerald is dead. He cannot hurt Maria."

"He may have already hurt her, Santos," replied Essie.

"Please, Miss Essie," argued the young man. "Give me more time." He looked directly into Essie's eyes as he clutched her hands tightly.

"Oh, all right," agreed Essie. "I guess a few more hours won't make a difference. And finding her name tag does seem to indicate that she ran into the woods... just not where she is now. I will make some more phone calls. And Santos..."

"I go back to kitchen," he said, now moving towards her door. "Maria will come back for baby. I know." He nodded continuously as he looked back at Essie. She followed him into the hallway where he abruptly turned back and with an embarrassed downward glance, briefly leaned over the handlebars of her walker and hugged her tightly. Essie heard a door open as she felt some snowflakes from Santos's jacket melt against her blouse. Santos leaned back. "Sorry, Miss Essie. No mean get you wet!"

"It's okay, Santos," she replied as the young man turned and quickly disappeared down the hallway. The sound of a doorway slammed and Essie turned to her left just in time to see Clara Monroe's door close. Oh, no! she thought, just what I need! That old busybody will concoct some new story now!" She stormed back into her apartment and closed her door behind her, panting with worry.

Chapter Twenty

"Getting a burp out of your little thing is probably the greatest satisfaction I've come across. It's truly one of life's most satisfying moments."
–Brad Pitt

Trying not to think what would happen if Clara had seen one of the Happy Haven kitchen workers give her a totally innocent hug, Essie put that possibility away and decided to concentrate on the issues at hand. Desperate situations call for desperate measures, thought Essie, as she went to her chair and sat back down. She couldn't help but notice the items on her end table that reflected all of her pressing problems–Maria's wallet with her green card, the gift box with the expensive necklace from Hubert Darby, and her open telephone directory. At the moment, she couldn't do anything about the first two items, but maybe she could let her fingers do the walking through her directory to see if she could find out some more information about the missing mother of baby Antonio.

Looking in the section where local government office numbers were listed, Essie quickly found a number for the Reardon Police Department. She was a resident of Reardon, she thought to herself, and she could report information and ask for information as well as any other resident. She quickly pressed the numbers indicated and an operator answered promptly.

"I'd like to talk to someone about a recent traffic fatality," she began. She really had no idea what she was going to say or even if anyone would talk to her about the accident, but she decided that it was worth a try.

"Traffic Investigation," announced the operator and informed her to wait as she transferred her to the appropriate department. Soon a male voice responded.

"Phelps," said the man. "Reardon PD."

"Oh, yes," said Essie, "I'm calling about a recent traffic fatality. The victim was Gerald Compton. It happened last night."

"Yeah," replied the officer. "How can I help you?"

"I'm just calling to see if you have any information about his . . . uh, his next of kin?"

"Uh . . . yeah . . . just a minute, let me find that file. Okay, here. Yeah, the father is the next of kin . . . a Harold Compton. You can direct any inquiries to him. You need a number for him?" The officer sounded harried.

"No," said Essie as politely as possible. "I was wondering about his wife."

"Uh, don't have a record for a wife," replied Officer Phelps, apparently looking through his records. "Just the father."

"So, you don't have any indication of what happened to Gerald Compton's wife Maria?" she said, pressing him.

"No," he said, somewhat befuddled. "The father identified the body. That was it. Never mentioned a wife."

"May I ask what prompted you to contact the father?"

"Listen, lady," said Phelps, "what's this all about? You a relative?"

"I'm just trying to locate his wife," she replied. "She's been missing since the accident."

"You wanta report her as a missing person?" asked Phelps.

"No," said Essie. "I'm just curious why the father didn't mention Gerald's wife or report her missing."

"Hey," said Phelps, casually, "maybe she isn't missing. Who knows? But, lady, if you want to report her missing, you need to come down to . . ."

"Uh, no, thank you, Officer," replied Essie, "I'm sure she'll turn up soon." She gently replaced the receiver. Now what to do? Other than Santos and her friends and herself, no one seemed to care what had happened to Maria Compton. The young woman had no relatives in Reardon or anywhere for all they knew. None of the people who cared about her had any authority to force the police to pursue an investigation. And, of course, it hadn't even been twenty-four hours since she had been missing. She had often heard that someone had to be missing at least twenty-four hours before the police would even consider them missing. And Maria had no relatives in Reardon (except her baby) to officially file a missing person's report. Where could the young woman be? If she was dead, her body had not been found. At least, no body had been reported. How could she have just disappeared from her apartment last night?

A soft cry alerted Essie to baby Antonio, beginning to stir on her bed. She quickly gathered the paraphernalia that she needed to feed the youngster and headed into her bedroom. She settled herself on her bed and gathered the infant onto her lap and squirted a small amount of liquid into his mouth. The hungry baby began to suck immediately on the little rubber finger.

"Where's your mommy?" Essie whispered to Antonio as she cuddled and fed him.

The baby responded only with pleasant gurgling noises as he stared up into Essie's eyes. Essie was soon entranced with his sweet face and thoughts of his family predicament faded as she bonded with the bundle in her arms.

After a half hour or so, Essie placed the contented and newly changed baby back on her bed. She rolled herself out to her living room and landed exhausted in her chair. She was now getting hungry and she looked over at the present from Hubert Darby and was actually annoyed that it wasn't peanut brittle. She could use a little sweet treat right about now. Maybe she had something to chew on in her pocketbook she thought as she scooted over to her desk and began rummaging through the items in her purse.

There was a sharp knock on the door. It didn't sound like one of the nurses, who would typically knock quickly and then open the door. Her friends would do the same. But, of course, it wouldn't be any of her friends at the door as the building was under quarantine. Surely, her children weren't here this early. They had said five o'clock and it was barely three thirty. Essie cautiously shuffled over to the door and peeked out.

Violet Hendrickson was standing in the hallway, her companion clipboard and pencil tucked professionally under her arm. As with all staff members during the virus outbreak, she wore a green paper face mask which only added to the woman's frightening appearance.

"Miss Essie," began Violet, her sharp voice somewhat muffled by the mask. "Have you been entertaining the kitchen workers in your apartment?"

"What?" sputtered Essie. "What do you mean 'entertaining'?"

"You know what I mean, Essie," said Violet, glaring at her through the crack in the door. "Are you having male kitchen workers in your apartment?"

"Miss Hendrickson!" exclaimed Essie. "Are you suggesting that I–a ninety-year-old woman–would be engaging in romantic activities with the help?" Essie knew, of course, what Violet was speaking about.

Obviously, Clara Monroe had been complaining again. After Clara had seen Santos give her that hug a while ago, she had probably contacted Violet and lodged another complaint. It was actually funny, thought Essie, that Clara would even begin to imagine that she–Essie–would be having a tryst with someone Santos's age.

"It has been reported," continued Violet Hendrickson, "that men . . . men who are known to work in the kitchen . . . have been seen coming out of your apartment. It has also been reported that said men have been seen embracing you!"

"I'm a very friendly person!" retorted Essie. "I embrace a lot of people! I've even been known to embrace a plumber or too in my time when they unclogged a toilet for me! They never seem to get the recognition they deserve for their service, don't you agree, Miss Hendrickson?"

"Don't change the subject, Essie," said Violet with a cold smirk that Essie could still clearly see over her mask. "You can't laugh this off. We have rules here at Happy Haven. We have standards to uphold. We will not tolerate residents comingling with staff!" Violet gave a sharp little upwards jerk of her chin.

"I can assure you, Miss Hendrickson," replied Essie, attempting to stand up to her full four feet three inches. "I can assure you that I have never conmen . . . or commenced . . . or whatever you are suggesting. And you can tell that busybody Clara Monroe to mind her own business and keep her door shut!"

"Really, Essie," said Violet, shaken from Essie's defense of her morals, "Miss Monroe can hardly help but notice inappropriate behavior that occurs right outside of her doorstep!"

"Inappropriate behavior!" cried Essie, her sides hurting from the laugh that demanded to come forth. "Kidnapped kangaroos! I'll show Clara some inappropriate behavior if that's what she's looking for! If I gave Clara a friendly hug, she'd probably think I was attacking her!"

Violet took a calming breath. She orchestrated this breathing with her hands, gently raising and lowering them like a band leader attempting to quiet a rowdy trombone section. "Essie," she said finally, carefully replacing a wayward lock that had come loose from her very tight hairdo. "There's no need to get hysterical."

"I'm not hysterical, Miss Hendrickson," whispered Essie to the Happy Haven Director. "It's Clara Monroe who's hysterical. She thinks anyone and everyone's behavior is designed to annoy her. Believe me, that is not so. I'll tell you what she saw . . . Miss Hendrickson. Um . . . one of the workers brought me some ice cream and I . . . um . . . gave him a tip because I had heard his family was suffering financially. He was grateful so he gave me a hug . . . a very chaste hug right in the middle of the hallway. That's what Clara saw."

"Humph," declared Violet. "I suppose it's possible that Clara exaggerated . . . ." Violet fidgeted with her clipboard and twisted the tip of her elegant high heel into the carpet.

"It's more than possible," urged Essie. "It's her daily behavior. She sees scandal everywhere." Essie waved her hands about in a fury to indicate Clara's activities. "As a matter of fact, she's probably listening to us speaking right now, and she'll no doubt distort our conversation so much that it will be all over Happy Haven that you and I are . . . thespians or homo sapiens . . . or something worse before the day is out!"

"My goodness!" declared Violet, quickly stepping back a space from Essie's walker. "All right, Essie. I will let it go this time. But, please, be careful what you do, and remember who lives next door." With a glance over her shoulder to the left at Clara's door, she gave a disgusted little roll of her eyes that Essie could see above her face mask and strode quickly down the hallway, her high heels soundless on the carpet, but the kick pleat on her tight skirt slapping the backs of her thighs as a sort of dramatic punctuation.

Chapter Twenty-One

"I figure that if the children are alive when I get home, I've done my job."
—Roseanne Barr

As soon as Essie retreated back into her apartment, the phone rang again. It's amazing that baby Antonio is able to sleep through all the racket, thought Essie. She grabbed the receiver on the second ring and greeted the caller.

"Essie," said the familiar voice of Opal. "At the risk of setting you off again . . ."

"Opal, I'm sorry," said Essie. She had been unnecessarily curt with her friend the last time they had spoken.

"It's fine, Essie," replied Opal, calmly. "What's this I hear about Hubert Darby giving you a Kriegsted necklace?"

"I see Marjorie wasted no time in spreading the word," replied Essie as she collapsed into her chair. "What am I going to do, Opal?"

"Describe this necklace to me, Essie," demanded Opal, "and tell me exactly what it looks like."

"It's just like I told Marjorie," said Essie, "it's a gold pendant on a gold chain."

"Does it look real?" asked Opal.

"I don't know, Opal," replied Essie, annoyed. "I'm not one for fancy jewelry. I'm not sure I'd know real from fake if my life depended on it."

"Hold it up to a light," said Opal.

"And what's that going to prove?" asked Essie. "I wrapped it back up in the paper. I'm going to return it to Hubert as soon as the quarantine is lifted."

"Essie, that necklace could be worth a lot of money!"

"All the more reason to return it!" Essie exclaimed. "I can't take an expensive gift from Hubert Darby. I barely know the man!"

"Yes," agreed Opal. "You are the epitome of propriety, Essie. You with that little secret swaddled in your bedroom."

"Stop it, Opal!" chided Essie. "I'm trying to do what's right. Taking care of this baby while we search for his mother is right. Accepting expensive jewelry from Hubert Darby is not right."

"Fine! Fine!" replied Opal. "I don't know what I can do about either of these problems, Essie from my room. I wish I could be there to help you care for Antonio. Is he doing well?"

"Yes, Opal," said Essie, "he's fine. I'm just in a tizzy trying to keep him a secret from people."

"Is anyone else suspicious?" asked Opal.

"Clara," replied Essie, "of course. She's suspicious of the postman."

"You are the lucky one having her for a neighbor," said Opal, commiserating.

"Yes," agreed Essie. "She caught Santos giving me a little hug out in the hallway a bit ago and imagined we were having some wild tempestuous affair and immediately reported it to Violet!"

"No!" exclaimed Opal.

"Yes!" said Essie. "And of course Violet was at my door in an instant to scold me for fraternizing with the help."

"She didn't see Antonio, did she?" asked Opal, aghast.

"No!" said Essie. "I managed to keep her in the hallway and, luck would have it, Antonio was asleep."

"Thankfully, newborns tend to sleep most of the time," said Opal.

"Yes," said Essie, "thankfully. If he were older, he'd surely be more demanding and I wouldn't have a minute to rest. I wouldn't have a minute to sit here and chat with my friends."

"Okay, Essie," said Opal, "I get the message. I just called because Marjorie told me you were worried about this necklace that Hubert gave you and she thought I could help."

"I'm sorry, Opal," replied Essie, chagrinned. "Do you really think this necklace is worth a lot of money?"

"If it's from Kreigsted's and not just in a Kreigsted's box," suggested Opal, "then from how you describe it, it could be worth thousands of dollars."

"Thousands!" cried Essie.

"Yes, Essie!" replied Opal, severely. "If that's 24 carat gold in the necklace . . . I'd say you're talking many thousands of dollars."

"I wish you could see this necklace, Opal," said Essie, wistfully. "Maybe I'm imagining it."

"I could tell you, Essie," said Opal, "if I could just see the necklace. I do fancy myself somewhat of a jewelry expert. As you know, I have this opal that . . ."

"Yes, yes," replied Essie petulantly. "I do wish you could look at it, but how am I supposed to get it to you to show you? Nobody is allowed to be out and about because of the quarantine."

"None of the residents, you mean," said Opal. "You could have one of the staff members bring it up to me. Maybe that Santos, the one who conned you into caring for baby Antonio? Surely, he could run a . . . uh . . . Christmas present from your place up to mine?"

"Hmm," said Essie, thinking aloud. "Let me consider that. I've had him chasing all over the place looking for Maria. The poor man barely has time to do his kitchen duties let alone have a life of his own."

"It's his fault!" cried Opal. "He could have . . . should have turned that baby over to the authorities the minute he realized his mother was not going to return when she said she would!"

"His heart's in the right place, Opal," argued Essie. "Besides, that isn't the question. The question for you is what to do about the necklace . . . and Hubert Darby."

"Yes, your swain," replied Opal, deadpan. Sometimes, Essie had difficulty determining whether or not Opal was teasing her.

"What was Hubert thinking of?" Essie responded with a moan. "He barely speaks to me."

"He obviously has feelings for you," said Opal, "and he obviously has more money than any of us had ever imagined if that necklace is worth what I think it is."

"Maybe I should call him and discuss this with him," pondered Essie.

"I'd say just wait until they lift the quarantine and then return it to him and explain your reasoning. It's probably better to do this in person," said Opal.

"I guess you're right," said Essie. "How did I get myself in this predicament?"

"I guess by being so irresistible to men, Essie," noted Opal, dryly.

"Holy gladiola, Opal!" cried Essie, "that's the last thing I am!"

"No man has offered me any expensive jewelry since I've been living at Happy Haven," noted Opal, a bit wistfully.

"Stop! We don't know for sure it's expensive!" said Essie. "I'm going on the premise it's costume jewelry until I find out otherwise."

"I'd be glad to provide you with that assurance," said Opal confidently, "if you'll just have your new boyfriend bring that necklace up to my place for an appraisal."

"He's not my boyfriend!" cried Essie. "How can he be, when I'm obviously taken by Hubert?" Essie laughed at her own predicament. It was a good thing her husband John was not alive to hear her discussing, not one but, two 'boyfriends'! "I'll do what I can, Opal." They both hung up and Essie contemplated whether or not she should bother Santos again while he was working in the kitchen. Another phone call settled the issue for her.

"Miss Essie," said the now familiar voice of the young man who had started the entire baby fiasco. "I take smoke break. I check with you. See if you find more about Maria."

"No, Santos," she replied, "I haven't found anything new that might help us locate her. I think your finding her name tag in the woods near her apartment is our best clue so far. It tells us she was there recently, but is no longer. At the moment, we're at a roadblock. And we . . . or rather I have another . . . little problem that you may be able to help me with."

"Yes, Miss Essie," he said. "I can help you with problem."

"My family is coming over tonight at five o'clock to take me out to dinner," she reported over the phone. "Obviously, I can't leave Antonio alone. I tried to put them off, but they are determined. And my friends can't watch him because they're all quarantined!"

"I can help, Miss Essie," he said. "I take Antonio to supply closet while you go to dinner with family!" His apparent pride in his idea was audible in his voice.

"Would you?" she asked with joy. "That would certainly solve the problem, and we could keep Antonio's existence a secret a bit longer. Maybe Maria will return by tomorrow."

"I hope so, Miss Essie," said Santos. "What time I come to your apartment to get Antonio?"

"Maybe around 4:30?" she asked.

"Si, Miss Essie, is no problemo!"

"Oh, and Santos," she added, "there is one other little errand I'd like you to perform for me if you wouldn't mind."

"Miss Essie," said Santos, "I do all your errands. You need Santos do your lavandos? Your laundry?"

"No, Santos," she replied smiling over the phone, "something much easier. Can you come to my apartment for just a moment? I'll explain when you get here."

"I be there fast fast, Miss Essie!" said the young man. He said good-bye and hung up.

"I'd better get going!" said Essie to herself with a huff. "Of all the times Claudia would choose to take me out, she had to pick the one day when I'm in the middle of a major crisis."

Essie glanced at her watch and saw that it was after four in the afternoon. She had less than an hour to get ready before her three children–Prudence, Claudia, and Kurt–arrived to whisk her off to Antonio's Italian Restaurant, and, no, the irony of the fact that her favorite Italian restaurant shared the same name as the little boy asleep on her bed was not lost on her.

I'd better be sure I have everything ready for Santos to take care of Antonio, she thought. She quickly rolled to her kitchen and cleaned out one of the glove bottles and filled it with fake formula. She got out a sack from under her sink and filled it with an extra bottle that Marjorie had supplied from her stock and five or six pairs of make-shift diapers. She then scooted to her bedroom and selected a nice outfit to wear to dinner and returned to her living room where she sat on her sofa and slowly changed from her everyday trousers and pull-on shirt into a nicer pair of dress pants and fancy blouse. Putting on the outfit was difficult without the help of one of her aides, but today she attempted it herself because she didn't want any staff members in her apartment any longer than was necessary—in case they discovered Antonio's presence. When she was dressed and had Antonio's overnight bag packed and waiting by the doorway, she headed into her bedroom with a full glove bottle, because she knew it would soon be time for the little fellow to wake up and when he did . . . he'd be hungry!

Chapter Twenty-Two

"What good mothers and fathers instinctively feel like doing for their babies is usually best after all."
–Dr. Benjamin Spock

Like clockwork, baby Antonio was soon stirring and Essie transferred him to his walker basket and rolled back to the living room where she ensconced herself and the infant in her lounger to enjoy their time together. Antonio quickly finished off the bottle he had started earlier and Essie and the infant were soon locked together in a delightful "conversation" while she waited for an appropriate number of burps and the eventual filling of the pants. She held the tot over her shoulder and gently rocked him back and forth. Antonio cooed and his tiny head wobbled around as he seemed to be taking in the sights and sounds nearby. Essie inhaled the relaxing odor of the holiday incense still wafting around her living room. She wondered if Antonio found its smell as calming as she did. The little fellow did seem remarkably relaxed and happy. Maybe those wise men were on to something, mused Essie. Frankincense and myrrh may just be the ideal aromas for calming babies. Antonio's head turned to Essie's end table and his gaze was suddenly fixated on the golden necklace from Hubert Darby that Essie had left sitting on top of its gift box and wrapping paper. She looked at the baby's eyes as the sparkle from the necklace reflected in his pupils. Gold, frankincense, and myrrh! Ah, yes! The three traditional Christmas gifts for a Christmas baby. And this baby seemed to be enjoying them all.

Enough reverie, Essie thought. As she rocked and hummed to the baby, she thought about the next few hours and how she would handle them. She really didn't want to go out anywhere tonight, but her children were insistent and her son Kurt didn't get to come down to see her all that often, so she felt obligated to spend time with him when he was in town. Of course, she would see him on Christmas–she would see all of her children and grandchildren–but she really wanted to spend some extra time with her only son away from all the hustle and bustle of a huge family get-together that would occur on Christmas day at Claudia's.

A soft knock on the door alerted her. Santos stuck his head in. When she saw his masked face, she motioned him inside and gestured for him to close the door behind him.

"Miss Essie," he whispered, pulling down his face mask, "Baby awake! Santos come quick, quick! Help Miss Essie."

"Santos, here take this!" said Essie, reaching over to her end table and picking up the golden necklace. As she lifted it over the baby's head, little Antonio followed the jewelry with his entire face. "Santos, can you please take this necklace up to Miss Opal in B227? She's expecting it."

"Very nice gift," said Santos, carefully taking the necklace from Essie. "You want to put in box, Miss Essie?"

"Oh, no!" replied Essie, "it's not a gift. It's a problem . . . oh . . . it's too complicated to explain . . . but I want Opal to examine . . . to look at it. She's more knowledgeable about these things than I am."

"Yes, Miss Essie," said Santos, cautiously holding the delicate chain and pendant with both hands. "I take to Miss Opal. B227?"

"Yes, B227," she said. "Thank you, Santos."

"I go, Miss Essie. I be back for baby at 4:30."

Santos quickly slipped out of Essie's apartment, leaving Essie alone. She saw that Antonio was starting to get sleepy so she put him back in his basket and rolled him back to her bedroom and wrapped him tightly in his blankets and set him on her bed. She sat next to him and hummed to him gently. Soon the infant was fast asleep. Essie returned to her living room and had barely sat back down in her chair when her telephone rang.

"Essie," said Opal, when Essie answered the phone, "this necklace is quite lovely. It certainly looks like real gold to me."

"So it's not just costume jewelry?" asked Essie.

"No," she said. "Either Hubert Darby is wealthy and knows he's giving you an expensive piece of jewelry or he's in possession of this necklace and has no idea what it's worth."

"What do you think it's worth?" probed Essie.

"If it's twenty-four carat gold, which it looks like to me," suggested Opal, "I'd say it's worth several thousands of dollars. Maybe ten thousand. Maybe even twenty thousand!"

"Popping pandas!" exclaimed Essie. "What's the matter with that man? Why would he do this? And he led me to believe it was a box of peanut brittle!"

"He probably thought you wouldn't accept it if you knew it was expensive jewelry!" said Opal.

"And he would have been right!" answered Essie. "I wonder if he gives things like this to all of the women he's courted."

"Essie," said Opal, "I thought you knew. Everyone says that Hubert is a bachelor. He's never been married. Some residents think he's never even had a girlfriend . . . or woman friend. You're his first!"

"Lucky me!" whined Essie. "I don't want or need a boyfriend!"

"Not even a rich one?" asked Opal.

"No!" retorted Essie. "I'm perfectly happy the way things are. I'm happy to be Hubert's friend. I'm happy to be friends with many people, but I'm not looking for anything else. What a mess!"

"I'm sorry, Essie," replied Opal. "Shall I have Santos bring the necklace back to you?"

"Is he still there?" asked Essie, incredulous that Opal would force the young man to wait while the two of them chatted about such a personal matter.

"No, Essie," said Opal, "but I can call him and have him come back up to my room."

"Let me think," said Essie. "If I talk to Santos and he has time, I may have him go up and get the necklace and bring it back to me. But, there's no reason to rush to do that now. It's not as if I can give it back to Hubert today. Not with the quarantine. I'm certainly not going to have Santos deliver it to Hubert. I need to speak to Hubert myself–face to face."

"I'd like to be there to see that," said Opal, slyly.

"Well, I'm not going to do it in public," said Essie. "I don't want to mortify the poor man."

"Of course," replied Opal, "I mean, the loss of your affection will be a terrible blow to him."

"Stop it, Opal!" chided Essie. "I don't know how . . . serious he is . . . about me. Eeee chickens! It sounds like we're high schoolers!"

"Not many high school boys can afford jewelry from Kreigsted's," noted Opal.

"Why is this happening now?" cried Essie. "My family will be here shortly to take me to dinner."

"Oh my!" exclaimed Opal. "What are you going to do about Antonio?"

"Santos is going to pick him up and keep him in the storage closet until I return," said Essie.

"Why not have Santos bring him up to me?" suggested Opal. "I'd be happy to watch him until you return."

"I'll see, Opal," replied Essie. "It's really what Santos can do conveniently with the baby without anyone finding out that he has Antonio. I'm not sure it's safe for him to cart the baby up to the second floor. It's not like he has an enclosed basket in a walker that he uses to get places."

"Okay," said Opal, "but the offer stands. Just let him know that I'm here . . . and I'm sure Marjorie or Fay would watch him in their rooms too."

"Yes," said Essie, "I'm sure. We'll see what works. The fewer people who know about the baby and the fewer people who see him, the better. Thank you, Opal, for examining the necklace. It helps to know exactly what I'm dealing with . . . even if it's not what I wanted to hear."

"You're welcome, Essie," said Opal. The friends ended their call and Essie looked at her watch only to realize that it was almost time for her children to arrive to take her out to dinner. Santos would be here to pick up the baby shortly before they came. Essie headed into her small bathroom for a few last minute ablutions and a brief potty stop. She examined her face in the mirror and judged herself sufficiently clean to be seen in public. That was actually the only criteria–cleanliness–that really mattered much these days to Essie.

She rolled back into her living room just as her telephone rang.

"Curdling gerbils," she exclaimed, "that telephone has rung more since they instituted that quarantine than it ever did before. It's a good thing I'm not sick with that horrible virus or I'd never have enough peace and quiet to get well." She plopped down in her chair and grabbed the receiver.

"Mom!" said Claudia into the phone. "We're so sorry! We can't make it!"

"What?" exclaimed Essie. "Why?"

"Do you have your television on?" asked Claudia. "Have you looked out your window?"

"No," said Essie to her youngest daughter, "what's wrong?"

"Just the snowstorm of the century!" replied Claudia with excitement. "No one is going out in this mess. Most places of business have closed. We just checked. Antonio's closed hours ago. There's virtually no restaurant anywhere in Reardon open now. It's even doubtful that we could get to Happy Haven."

"Jumpin' pumpkins!" exclaimed Essie, "I had no idea!"

"It's true," continued Claudia, "they have snowplows out, but even they're having trouble getting around. Most government offices are closed. Only police emergency workers are out. How are you doing, Mom? I know you're under quarantine. Is there enough staff there to get meals to everyone? I worry about you stuck in your room."

"I . . . I . . . don't know," she answered. "I haven't heard anything. They've been making announcements and giving updates about the quarantine, but this is the first I've heard about a snowstorm."

"Well, if you don't believe me," said Claudia, "just take a look outside your window. It's a mess!"

Essie glanced over to her window. The blinds were drawn so she could just see a glimmer of light peeking around the edges of the window.

"Yes, dear," said Essie to her daughter, "I'll check on it. But, don't worry about me. I'm safe and sound . . . and warm! They bring our meals. Yes, it's boring being here all alone," she lied. She was anything but bored, but at the moment it was better if Claudia believed that she was fine and out of mischief, "but I have my puzzles to keep me busy."

"That's good!" replied Claudia. "What would you do without your puzzles? Maybe we can do an outing in a day or two when this front clears through. Kurt won't be leaving until after Christmas."

"Yes, dear," said Essie, "that would be lovely. Say hello to Kurt for me."

"I will, Mom," replied Claudia. "Take care!" Essie quickly hung up her telephone and pushed herself up and out of her chair. She quickly rolled her walker over to her window and tugged on the pulley to raise the blinds. Outside, all that was visible was a swirling sheet of white. She couldn't even see the other wing of Happy Haven across the courtyard. It was a complete white-out. It was a good thing because it meant that her family would not be coming to take her away from the baby she needed to watch. It was a bad thing because it was terrible weather for anyone to be out in . . . and Essie hoped that did not include Antonio's mother Maria.

Chapter Twenty-Three
"A person's a person, no matter how small."
–Dr. Seuss

A reprieve! thought Essie. Here she had thought her major problem would be just going out to dinner with her family and getting back without anyone finding out about baby Antonio. Now she didn't have to worry about that. Now she had to switch gears, so to speak, and consider what her next step would be if Maria wasn't found soon–very soon. Should she continue to attempt to hide the baby and search for his mother or should she reveal his presence and ask for help from the authorities? With this terrible snowstorm going on, she doubted the police could do much to search for Maria even if Essie did report her missing. Please let Maria be safe, she prayed. Probably all she could reasonably do until the storm subsided was to keep Antonio safe and warm, and that she resolved to do. Tomorrow would be soon enough to let anyone else know about her little charge.

The PA system crackled to life again. It was beginning to seem like a train station at Happy Haven with these constant audio interruptions. First the quarantine and now another message in the middle of the afternoon. So uncharacteristic for her facility! The calm voice of Phyllis came over the microphone:

"Residents, if you haven't noticed already by looking out your windows or by hearing about it on television, our area is in the grips of a major winter snowstorm. The governor has declared a state of emergency and has requested that only necessary vehicles be on the road until further announcements. Because this storm came up so suddenly and because of its severity, we're experiencing some staffing problems here at Happy Haven. We promise that we will not let these difficulties inconvenience you, our residents. Some of our staff have not been able to get here due to conditions of the roads. Also, some of our staff who are already here are not able to leave for the same reason. We've made arrangements for our staff to sleep here overnight tonight by setting up makeshift beds in the dining hall. As the quarantine is still in effect, the dining hall is not in use, so this should not present a hardship to any of our residents. Our staff will still continue to bring your meals to your rooms and the nurses' aides who are presently in the building will cover for those who haven't been able to get here. It may take us a bit longer than usual to accomplish everything tonight, but we will get to all of you. Please be patient. If you have an emergency, you can call the front desk and we will assist you. In the mean time, remain in your rooms and stay safe and warm."

Fiddling figs! thought Essie. That probably meant that Santos would be spending the night in the dining hall with the other staff members who were still working. She wondered if her nighttime aide Lorena had made it in to work before the emergency road travel restriction was implemented. She tried to remember what Lorena had said to her in the past about what time she usually arrived at work. It was obviously sometime in the late afternoon. If Lorena showed up at or near her regular time and Essie was already for bed, Lorena would be even more suspicious than she had been last night. If Lorena had not made it to work, Essie might be able to get ready for bed and just have Lorena's replacement give her her nighttime meds and be on her way. The less time any staff member spent in her apartment, the less likely it would be that they'd discover Antonio, assuming he was sleeping when her aide arrived. It would be more difficult now since Essie was alone without any of her three pals to hide the baby in her bedroom.

Baby Antonio, possibly realizing that she was thinking about him, cried out softly from her bedroom. Essie glanced at her watch. Hmmm, he'd only been asleep a little over an hour. She quickly headed to the other room and collected the small bundle and put him in his basket and then returned to her living room where she grabbed the last of her prepared glove bottles and lowered herself back into her chair and began to nurse the baby. Antonio gulped the formula hungrily. Lucky, thought Essie, no quarantine or snowstorm seemed to affect his appetite.

A soft knock on the door was followed by Santos peeking his head in. He wore the de rigeur green face mask this time and was carrying a plastic food tray with a metal plate cover on top. When Essie saw the young man, she again motioned for him to quickly enter. Santos moved into the living room and quietly closed the door behind him. He immediately set the tray and plate cover by the doorway.

"Miss Essie," he began breathlessly, "you not go dinner with family? Big snowstorm!"

"Yes, Santos," she responded, "I know about it! My daughter called me and told me they couldn't get here. I see you have a cover story if anyone asks why you were in my apartment." She nodded to the tray and plate cover he had just set down. "I'll keep Antonio tonight. I don't think you'll need to hide him in the closet."

"Very good, Miss Essie," said Santos. "All workers stay here at Happy Haven tonight. We cannot go home! Very bad snow! My sports car cannot go in snow."

"I know, Santos," she replied. "I heard the announcement. I hear they're setting up sleeping bags and cots for the staff members who are still here."

"Si," he said, "we all sleep in dining hall. We cannot go out in snowstorm."

"That's wise," she said. "Santos, do you know Lorena? I can't remember her last name. She's one of the nurses's aides."

"Miss Lorena," said the young waiter, "si, I know. She very funny lady. She makes me laugh!"

"That's good," responded Essie. "Do you happen to know if she's here? Did she make it in to work?

She's my night time aide and if she's here, I assume she'll be around to do my evening meds. I'm afraid she's a bit suspicious of me from my behavior in hiding Antonio last night."

"I can hide baby, Miss Essie," said Santos, "when Miss Lorena bring you pills."

"That's just it," said Essie. "I don't know if she's here, and if she is, when she'll be here, assuming she'll probably have to take over the duties of other aides. Of course, if she isn't here, I may be able to cover with her replacement. But if anyone shows up when Antonio is awake or while I'm feeding him, there would be no way to keep him secret if that person came into my apartment."

"Si, Miss Essie," he said. "It is very difficult. I take baby now to storage closet?" The young man looked hesitantly at the older woman as the infant continued to suck away at the yellow rubber glove in her arms.

"No," she replied finally, "let's not rock the boat."

"Rock boat?" Santos asked. "You mean rock baby, Miss Essie?"

"No, it's an expression, Santos," she explained. "It means let's not cause any more . . ."

"Congojá!" he cried.

"Si, I mean, yes," said Essie, "whatever that means, it sounds right!"

"Very good, Miss Essie," Santos said, edging closer to Essie's rocker and peering shyly at the little baby in her arms. "You take good care of baby Antonio, Miss

Essie. I am very smart to pick you to be baby's, how you say? Chacha?"

"After this, no more cha cha-ing for me, Santos!" chuckled Essie, looking down at the infant who smiled up into her face.

"I mean you are very good mother," he said, "Antonio is very happy baby." The woman and the young man continued to watch the infant sucking noisily at his dinner (or lunch). "You don't need speak good English to baby, Miss Essie."

"That's true," she agreed. "Now, when you go back to the kitchen, can you check to see if Lorena is here? If she is, can you call me or let me know. She's the only person I'm worried about. If she comes here to give me my meds while Antonio is awake, then she'll surely insist on informing Violet about him. We really need to be careful that we keep him hidden when she is here."

"I find Miss Lorena," said Santos, "and I find when she comes here to see you. I come get Antonio and take him to closet before Miss Lorena comes to your apartment, Miss Essie. You no worry! I can do!"

"Yes, I believe you can, Santos," said Essie. She marveled at how much the young man managed to do for this child in addition to fulfilling his regular duties. "You can touch him, you know." She smiled at Santos as the young man gingerly inched toward Essie's chair and cautiously reached his hand out and placed it on the baby's head.

"Baby is very warm," he said with a smile. "And . . . suave . . . soft."

"Yes," she agreed. "I think he knows you. You saved him, you know."

"No, you, Miss Essie," said Santos, pulling back. "You save baby."

"Let's consider it a joint effort," replied Essie, with a grin at her compatriot in crime. "Now, you'd better get going, before they miss you in the kitchen. And, be careful. Don't let anyone see you."

"Is okay if they see Santos," he said sticking out his lower lip. "I say I bring Miss Essie something to eat."

"Salubrious succotash!" she said, smacking her forehead with the palm of her hand. "I guess if I'm not going to dinner with my children, I will need you to bring me some dinner. As many times as you've been here to deliver me food, people are going to expect me to gain a lot of weight."

"Food is very good at Happy Haven," he replied, with a knowing nod, grabbing the tray and plate cover from near the doorway on his way out.

"And Santos," she called to him at the door, "would you have time to drop by Opal's apartment again and bring back that necklace?"

"Si, Miss Essie, I go get necklace. Bring supper. Santos can do all. No worry, Miss Essie." He listed his duties for himself on his fingers. "Do not forget, Miss Essie! It is Christmas! Very good time for everybody!"

"I hope you're right, Santos," replied Essie as Santos quietly slipped out her door. "You don't know how much trouble you've been causing," she whispered to Antonio who was only now slurping down the last few drops of fake formula. Essie tipped him upright and placed him over her shoulder. With a few gentle rocks and pats, a nice long burp erupted from the baby's tummy. "Good one, little man."

Another soft knock sounded on the door.

"That must be Santos back again," said Essie. "Grumpy Goodness! That was fast!" The knock repeated. Essie expected Santos to call out to her or open the door himself quietly. Most residents of Happy Haven typically kept their doors unlocked so that staff members could get in in case of emergencies. "Santos?" she called out softly. "The door is open. Come in."

The door creaked open a few inches. However, instead of the familiar face of her young Hispanic waiter, Essie saw the also familiar face of her next door neighbor and ultra-snoopy gossip–Clara Monroe. Clara looked inside and immediately honed in on Essie sitting in her rocker. Then, her eyes wandered down to Essie's lap, where baby Antonio was now being jostled contentedly. As Clara's eyes focused on the totally unexpected sight of a newborn infant in the arms of one of Happy Haven's elderly residents–with no accompanying relatives anywhere in sight–she pushed Essie's door back slowly and cautiously stepped into Essie's apartment. With her eyes still glued to the baby, she reached behind her and shut Essie's door without a word. Then, moving towards Essie, eyes still on the child, she finally opened her mouth.

"Essie Cobb! What are you doing with a baby?"

Chapter Twenty-Four

"The only creatures that are evolved enough to convey pure love are dogs and infants."
–Johnny Depp

Essie sat frozen. Clara Monroe in the middle of her living room was not what she was expecting at this moment. Things were going so well, she thought, and she had even escaped the major problem of having to go out to dinner with her children. Now, as swiftly as circumstances had calmed, they had erupted into crisis mode again. Essie stared at Clara and smiled sheepishly.

"Essie," demanded the small woman, "what are you doing with a baby here in your apartment? Oh, my! That's the noise I've been hearing! You've had this child in here since yesterday, haven't you?"

"I . . . I . . ." stuttered Essie. "Clara, what are you doing out of your apartment? There's a quarantine in effect!" Essie could see that there was no denying to Clara what her own eyes were telling her.

"I thought there was something funny going on!" declared the diminutive Clara with a punch of her fist, ignoring Essie's excuse. "I was right!"

"Clara," said Essie, with a puny laugh, "it's a rather funny story, actually." Essie gathered baby Antonio into her arms and began to rock him before he emitted any loud noise that might rile up Clara and just confirm her suspicions about her noisy neighbor. "It's actually rather sad too," she added.

Clara scowled. This was a no-nonsense woman, thought Essie, and the look on her face reminded her of a surly prison guard taking a recalcitrant prisoner off to execution. "Humph!" snorted Clara.

"I'd be glad to tell you, Clara," began Essie. Clara bunched up her upper lip and crossed her arms decisively.

"I bet you would, Essie Cobb," she said, pursing her lips together. "You have an excuse for every wild escapade you get involved with." She stabbed her index finger into Essie's face.

"Oh, Clara!" cried Essie, "Jingling Jezebels, this is no wild escapade!"

"It certainly looks like it!" replied Clara, edging closer to Essie's rocker and cautiously staring down at the infant in Essie's arms. "What in the world is that poor child sucking on?"

"It's a . . . well . . . it's actually a rubber glove that Opal turned into a bottle," Essie explained.

"Opal?" queried Clara, reaching out gingerly to touch the baby's feeding contraption. "You mean your tablemate? Is she involved in this baby snatching business too?"

"Clara!" exclaimed Essie, staring directly at Clara and shaking her head furiously. "There's no baby snatching involved. We . . . ."

"You and Opal?"

"Um . . . and Marjorie and Fay," added Essie.

"My God," declared Clara, "there's a gang of you involved in this! No wonder!" Clara shook her head. "And Santos? That young man who works in the kitchen?"

"You know Santos?" asked Essie.

"Of course," replied Clara, stomping over to Essie's sofa and sitting down on the edge like a hawk scouting prey from a mountain top. She continued to stare intently at the baby and his makeshift bottle. "I know everyone who works here. It always pays to be aware of the people and things around you. I knew you had something going on over here, Essie. I heard a lot of voices . . . far more than you usually have in your apartment." She again punctuated her remark with her bony finger.

"You got me, Clara!" replied Essie, with a shrug of her shoulders and a little laugh. "You found me out! I'm keeping a baby in here. So, I guess my question to you is, what are you going to do about it? Are you going to report me?"

"That's exactly what I should do, you know," said Clara, leaning in to the baby and reaching out to touch his chubby leg that was waving in the air. "You and your friends are breaking all the rules at Happy Haven. No one is supposed to have overnight visitors . . . and certainly no one is supposed to keep a baby in their apartment. Of course, that doesn't mean you can't have visitors . . . but I'm assuming this child is more than just the child of one of your relatives. I'm assuming he's been staying here with you overnight." Clara's eyes dared Essie to deny her statement.

"Yes, Clara, but there's a very good reason!" responded Essie. "His mother is . . ."

"His mother!" cried Clara. She puffed herself up to her full height, which wasn't much. "What mother would leave a newborn . . . and he does appear to be a newborn . . . with you? No offense, Essie, but why would his mother leave him with you . . . or anyone here at Happy Haven? None of us are equipped to care for children . . . especially newborns! What mother would do such a thing?"

"She's one of our kitchen workers," said Essie, "and she's disappeared. Santos and my tablemates and I have been trying to find her."

"What kitchen worker?" asked Clara, her tone changed, now all business.

"Her name is Maria Compton . . ."

"Oh, yes!" replied Clara, "I know who you mean. She always wears those bulky sweaters even when the dining hall is so warm. Oh, my! That's why! She didn't want anyone to know she was pregnant! I didn't even realize she was pregnant. I should have figured that out." Clara's hand went to her mouth and she chewed on her fingers as if doing so would assist her in figuring out a puzzle. Essie pondered the fact that Clara had noticed Maria and her predicament and she hadn't. Oh, well, she thought, I guess that's all part of being a gossip.

"Her husband was abusive," added Essie, in an attempt to ingratiate herself into Clara's good graces. "He beat Maria and the baby. See this gash on his cheek. It's almost healed. He has one on his leg too. That's where Gerald, the father, beat him. We know he beat Maria too. She was trying to get away from him. Santos was watching the baby for her last night while she went home to pack. But she never returned for the baby. Santos couldn't take Antonio . . ."

"The baby is Antonio?" asked Clara, as she tipped her head so she could look directly into the young boy's eyes.

"Yes," replied Essie. "Maria was supposed to come right back and get Antonio and Santos was keeping him in the supply closet, but she didn't return. He had no place to take Antonio because Santos lives in a boarding house and actually has less privacy than I do. So he asked me to assist him . . . and you know the rest . . . or you've figured out the rest."

"And this thing . . ." said Clara, pointing to the rubber glove device now sitting depleted on Essie's end table.

"Opal created it out of a new rubber cleaning glove," said Essie. "And Fay made some disposable diapers out of some adult diapers that . . . well, that all of us had."

"Oh my!" cried Clara suddenly. "What are you feeding him? Surely not regular milk? To a newborn?"

"No," said Essie, "of course not! We know better than that. We're giving him Vigor."

"That's that adult protein beverage, isn't it?" she asked.

"Yes, and I know it's not ideal..."

"It's a brilliant idea!" declared Clara. She snapped her fingers.

"You think so?" asked Essie, amazed that Clara actually seemed interested in the baby's care.

"Essie, I used to be a NICU nurse. The ingredients in some of those protein drinks might just be a reasonable substitute for baby formula. Of course, it's not as good as mother's milk, but no one here can provide him with that."

"That's for sure!" replied Essie, laughing and smiling cautiously at Clara. As her laughter subsided without any response from the severe Clara, Essie said, "Clara, can I please ask that you keep baby Antonio's presence here in my apartment a secret just a bit longer? I really will try to keep him as quiet as possible so you won't be disturbed..."

"Stop, Essie!" declared Clara with an accompanying stomp of her tiny feet on the ground. "You're not focusing on the real issue here."

Essie panicked as she wondered what Clara considered the real issue. Was she so consumed with propriety as Essie had believed that no matter what, she would report Essie and her little babysitting charge to Violet?

"And what is the real issue?" asked Essie, tentatively.

"Where is this child's mother and how do we find her?" said Clara.

"We? You mean you'll help us keep Antonio's presence a secret, Clara?" asked Essie.

"Someone has to help you!" replied Clara. "You surely aren't doing a very good job of it yourself. After all, I easily figured out that something was going on over here."

"True," agreed Essie. "So, Clara . . . what do you suggest we do to track down Maria Compton?"

"What have you done so far?" asked Clara, scooting closer to Essie. "Could I hold him just a bit?"

"Of course," said Essie. "Here." She lifted Antonio in the air and handed him to Clara. Antonio smiled up at Clara and gurgled. Clara accepted the infant with the ease and professionalism of a . . . well, of a seasoned former NICU nurse.

"Oh my," said Clara, "aren't you the handsome one! Look at all that hair!"

"Yes," said Essie, "and he doesn't seem to be missing his mother much."

"At this age, of course not," said Clara. "Now, where could his mother be? Tell me what you know."

"We don't know anything for sure," began Essie, "but we have surmised from various sources that after Maria left Antonio with Santos last night, she returned to her home and began to pack. We then believe her husband Gerald came home unexpectedly and they got into a fight. Maria ran out on foot and Gerald followed her in his car."

"And how do you know this?" asked Clara.

"We know Maria cannot drive," said Essie, "and we heard on television that Gerald Compton was killed in a car crash about that time."

"Oh dear! Poor little baby!" cried Clara, rocking Antonio close to her bosom while she patted his back gently.

"To be without a father, yes," said Essie, "but not to be without this father. He was a brute! Anyway, Santos searched Maria's apartment and found her wallet which we assume she left there in her hurry to get away. He also searched the area surrounding their apartment and found Maria's Happy Haven name tag. Maria hasn't reported in since last night and there was no mention of her in the news reports of Gerald's accident."

"Curious!" said Clara. "Go on."

"I checked with the local newspaper and with the place where Gerald worked. I actually spoke with his father. It appears the father didn't even believe in the legality of Gerald and Maria's marriage. No one at the place where he worked seemed to be aware that the two were married . . . if they were."

"This doesn't sound good," said Clara. "If the mother . . . this Maria Compton was anywhere where she could communicate, you would think her top priority would be to get to her baby . . . or at least get word to Santos where she was."

"Yes," said Essie, "that's why we're afraid that maybe she's injured or dead."

"Out on the side of a road somewhere," said Clara.

"Yes!" agreed Essie. "Or in the woods or some deserted place near her home. When she ran out on Gerald, she may have fallen."

"She may be injured!"

"Or dead," reiterated Essie.

"Yes," agreed Clara, "but the good news is that so far no one has reported discovering her body, so we have to proceed on the belief that she's out there somewhere and just can't make it back."

"That's what I'm thinking," said Essie, "that's what Santos is thinking too. He knows her well and he just doesn't believe Maria would desert her child."

"Certainly not this child," said Clara in a soft voice that Essie had never heard from her nosy neighbor. Clara beamed down at the infant in her arms.

"So, Clara," said Essie, "do you have any suggestions as to where we might look next? Where we might search for this little boy's mother?"

"I do," replied Clara, "the one obvious place you haven't looked. A hospital. If she's injured, she may have found her way to a local hospital . . . or possibly some Good Samaritan helped her get to an emergency room."

"But, Clara, if she's in a hospital," suggested Essie, "surely she'd call Santos and let him know she's all right."

"That's just it," said Clara. "She may not be all right. She may be in a hospital . . . unconscious or even in a coma!"

"Just like Bob Weiderley was!" declared Essie.

"Yes," said Clara, "and if she is, it's going to be a lot more difficult to track her down."

"Oh, no!" cried Essie. "We can't wait much longer before we're going to have to report Antonio."

"Then aren't you lucky you have Clara Monroe on your side!" said Clara, smiling at Essie over Antonio's little forehead.

"We certainly are!" replied Essie. "Thank you, Clara! You are certainly a revelation!"

"Enough, Essie!" said Clara. "Let's get to work! Give me your telephone book!"

"Coming up!" said Essie.

Chapter Twenty-Five
"It is the nature of babies to be in bliss."
–Deepak Chopra

Clara made haste in locating the main number for the nearest hospital and quickly dialed while Essie cuddled Antonio.

"Patient rooms," she announced in her sharp little voice when the operator answered. "I'd like the room of Maria Compton." She glanced at Essie as she waited for the operator to respond. "Hmm," she said in response to the voice on the other end. "No Maria Compton? Maybe I got the wrong hospital. Yes, thank you." She hung up and then spoke to Essie. "I can try other hospitals in the area, Essie, but something tells me that if the baby's mother was injured near here, she would have gone to or would have been taken to Reardon General. I'll check just in case."

As Essie continued to rock the baby and marvel that she was sitting in her living room being assisted in this secretive endeavor by her arch nemesis, Clara quickly used her finger to locate the main numbers for the three other hospitals in the Reardon area. Within a few minutes, it was obvious that Maria Compton was not a patient at any of them either.

"Don't lose heart, Essie," said Clara firmly. "I'm not done yet. It hasn't even been twenty-four hours since Maria went missing. She could still be out there undiscovered . . . ."

"Oh, Fred's heads, I hope not!" moaned Essie.

"Or," added Clara, philosophically, "she might be in a hospital but unable to contact anyone. She could be unconscious or injured so badly that she is unable to communicate. And, remember, you said she left her wallet in her apartment when she took off abruptly, so if she was in an accident and taken to a hospital and is unable to talk, the hospital staff has no way of knowing who she is."

"What would they do in that case?" asked Essie. She assumed Clara, as a former nurse, would be aware of procedures that would be followed.

"Of course, the staff would do everything they could to determine who she is," explained Clara, "but their first concern would be her health. They would be trying to stabilize her or deal with her injuries if she has any. Or if she's in a coma, then, of course, they can't ask her any questions. There are all sorts of possibilities. Once she's stabilized, they will certainly try to determine who she is."

"But that might not be for . . . ." Essie speculated.

"Well, not now, certainly," said Clara. She continued to clutch Essie's telephone as if it might inspire her to action.

"Can't we call the hospital and ask if they have a patient like Maria who is unidentified?" asked Essie.

"They won't give us information like that, Essie," said Clara.

"And neither will the police," replied Essie, "for the same reason. I guess we're stuck with trying to track her down ourselves and keeping Antonio hidden until we find her."

"This horrible snowstorm!" exclaimed Clara, as she rose and wandered over to Essie's window.

"I know," agreed Essie. "All I can think of is this poor baby's mama lying on the ground somewhere out in this weather."

"If I were younger, I'd put on my boots and winter coat and go out looking for her myself," said Clara. She pulled two of the blinds apart so she could get a better view of the swirling snow.

"Me too," said Essie. "But we can't do that. We're just going to have to do what we can do and that is to take care of the baby and try to find his mother in other ways."

Another soft knock at the door was followed by the door opening a crack and Santos popped his head in.

"Miss Essie?" he called out. When he saw Clara Monroe standing by Essie's window, he gasped and his eyes bulged out. "Miss Clara?"

"Come in, Santos," said Essie, waving him in. "Don't worry; Clara is on our side."

Santos moved into the room carrying his fake food tray. He gingerly moved over to Essie and was quickly joined by Clara. Clara popped back down on the sofa, beside Essie who was holding the baby.

"So, you're the source of all this brouhaha!" declared Clara in full investigatory mode.

"Miss Clara," began the young man, clutching the tray in front of him like a protective shield.

"Don't worry, Santos," Essie broke in, "Clara has been helping me try to locate Maria. I don't think we need to worry about her finding out about Antonio."

Santos' relaxed noticeably. His eyes softened and his shoulders dropped. "You find Maria, Miss Essie?" he asked anxiously.

"No," she replied sadly, "I'm afraid not. Clara checked all the local hospitals, but Maria is not registered as a patient in any of them. That doesn't mean she's not there."

"If she's unconscious," added Clara, "no one would know who she is. And I understand that you found her wallet with her identification . . ."

"Si," replied Santos, "Maria does not need any . . . you say . . . identification . . . but green card. Miss Essie has green card now. So no one knows who Maria is if she cannot talk."

"That's unfortunate," noted Clara, drumming her fingers nervously on the edge of Essie's sofa arm.

"We will continue to search for Maria," said Essie to Santos as she gently rocked Antonio. Santos stood forlornly before the two older women. "Santos, please don't lose faith. I can't help but believe that she's out there and that we will find her. In the mean time, we need to keep Antonio's presence quiet just a little longer. Did you find out anything about Lorena?"

"Si," replied Santos, "Miss Lorena comes to work on bus. She says she gets last bus before snow close the . . . everything!. Miss Lorena is not happy to stay here at Happy Haven all night on sleeping bag. She call husband. Husband not happy. Husband have to take care of children . . ."

"Yes, yes," interrupted Essie, "but Lorena is here and she will be making her rounds?"

"Si," said Santos, nodding. "But I hear Lorena say she is very busy and has to do other nurse's work too."

"So she might be here later? Or earlier?" asked Essie.

"I do not know, Miss Essie," he said.

"Essie," said Clara, "if you're worried about your night nurse's aide discovering Antonio, maybe we can work out an arrangement so I watch him while she's here. I do my own meds, so I don't have a night aide. You can bring him over to me."

"Si, Miss Clara! Very good!" said Santos, "but be very careful! Miss Violet watch hallways! She not want residents in hallways because of quarantine! Very bad!"

"We'll be careful, Santos," replied Essie, "but that does sound like a workable plan, Clara. And I won't have to bother you again, Santos."

"No bother Santos," the young man exclaimed. "I want to help baby Antonio. And Maria."

"It sounds to me, Santos," noted Clara, "that you have more than just friendly feelings towards this child's mother."

Santos blushed.

"Santos," cried Essie, "is this true? Are you sweet on Maria?" She rocked Antonio and wondered how much he looked like his mother.

"Si, I like Maria a lot, Miss Essie."

"Popping porcupines!" exclaimed Essie, "I certainly didn't see that. I just thought that . . . oh, never mind what I thought."

"But, Maria, she does not notice Santos," he added. "Maria only thinks about work and baby and getting away from bad husband."

"If she returns . . . ." began Clara.

"When she returns, Clara," said Essie, with a cautionary riveting of her forehead.

"When she returns, Santos," continued Clara, "maybe you can express your feelings to her." Essie was beginning to wonder if Clara was a gossip or a matchmaker.

"Si, Miss Clara," he said, "but first must find Maria. Very important. I am very worried for Maria."

"I know, Santos," said Essie, "we'll do everything we can to find Maria and help this innocent little baby." She smiled at Santos who returned her smile and took a deep breath.

"Oh, Miss Essie," he said suddenly, "I almost forget. Here is necklace back from Miss Opal." He reached into his pants pocket and brought out the gold necklace and handed it to her.

"Thank you, Santos," Essie replied taking the necklace with her free hand that was not holding the baby and placing it on her end table next to the Kreigsted box in which it had come.

"Miss Essie, Miss Clara," said Santos. "You want me to bring dinner here for you?"

Essie and Clara exchanged glances.

"Why not?" replied Essie. "I know we're breaking the quarantine, but I'm certainly not sick and it doesn't look as if Clara is either. So if we're careful not to be seen and you don't tell on us, Santos . . . ." Clara smiled and nodded.

"Santos not tell," he said. "I keep secret for you, ladies." With that, the young waiter grabbed his tray and plate topper and sneaked out of Essie's living room.

"It's so boring to eat alone," said Clara with a smile.

"Yes, it is!" agreed Essie.

"I see Santos brought you a present?" asked Clara, a small snicker beginning to develop at the corner of her mouth. She scooted closer to Essie's end table.

"Oh, that's not from Santos," said Essie, chuckling, when she realized that Clara was referring to the necklace. "It's from . . ."

"Goodness, Essie," said Clara, her eyes swelling. "I'm not an idiot! I recognize a Kreigsted box when I see one! Santos couldn't afford to buy anyone a gift from Kreigsted's. Someone has sent you this necklace a present?"

"Evidently," replied Essie, with a shrug. "Unfortunately."

"Unfortunately!" exclaimed Clara. "It's from Kreigsted's!"

"It is," Essie replied, "and that's why I can't accept it."

"You can't?"

"If you must know, Clara," said Essie, "it's from Hubert Darby! I'm certainly not going to accept an expensive gift from him!"

"Why not?"

"I barely know the man," responded Essie, leaning back in her rocker and cuddling Antonio over her shoulder. Clara gently touched the velvet box beside the necklace.

"Such a beautiful box!" declared Clara.

"You want to take a closer look?" asked Essie.

"Can I?" Clara asked, her eyes wide.

"I guess," replied Essie, pointing to it. Clara picked up the glittering necklace.

"Oh, my! Essie!" she said. "It's lovely! Hubert really must be smitten with you! This must have cost a fortune!"

"So Opal tells me," said Essie morosely.

"What?" asked Clara, confused.

"Hubert told me his gift was peanut brittle. It wasn't until I opened it and found this . . . this thing inside that I realized what he had really given me. I thought it might just be costume jewelry but I didn't know, so I had Santos take it up to Opal and she confirmed that it is truly real gold and from Kreigsted's. Or at least she thinks it is."

"Maybe Hubert doesn't know himself how much it's worth," suggested Clara.

"Maybe," said Essie. "Maybe it belonged to someone in his family. But if that's the case, that's even worse, because he shouldn't be giving me heirlooms . . . things that belonged to a loved one. I barely know the man. We just have friendly conversations. There's absolutely nothing romantic between us! Dappled apples! I'm over ninety! I don't want to be courted!"

"Then send him my way," said Clara, with a fluttering of her lashes.

"Clara!" cried Essie. "I thought you were the one who was so concerned with propriety! I can't believe we've lived next door to each other all these years and I'm just now getting to know you. There's obviously more to you than I thought!"

Chapter Twenty-Six
"Every baby born into the world is a finer one than the last."
–Charles Dickens

"Appearances can be deceiving," replied Clara, stretching back on Essie's sofa. "When I was a nurse, I was often privy to many family secrets that sometimes came out at very inopportune moments. Sometimes life and death moments! I know how to keep a secret, Essie. But, I must tell you, I really love knowing secrets too! There's just not much excitement going on around Happy Haven for me. Truth be told, I guess I'm a little jealous of you and how you managed to help poor Bob Weiderley. I pride myself on knowing what people are up to. Here you were solving that mystery for Bob and you–right next door to me–and I didn't even know it! How could that be?"

"It's good to know you like solving mysteries, Clara," said Essie. "I could use more help in tracking down Antonio's mother. I've pretty much tried every avenue I can think of."

"Anything else I can do to help find this sweet baby's mother," replied Clara, "count me in." She reached out her arms and Essie willingly handed Antonio over. The peaceful child smiled contentedly at Clara who cuddled him into her lap, her nursing experience evident.

"It's almost supper time and that means it's been almost twenty-four hours since Maria has been missing," noted Essie. "I'm thinking that I'll call the police again and find out exactly what we need to do to report a missing person. I think you have to be a relative. I wonder what they do when a person doesn't have a relative . . . or at least any relative that anyone is aware of."

"That would be a problem," agreed Clara, fixated on baby Antonio's face. The child followed Clara's face as she made funny and exaggerated expressions for him.

"You're wonderful with him, Clara," said Essie. So much for making snap judgments of people, she thought. Clara was certainly not the spoil-sport that she had envisioned her to be.

A tentative knock sounded on Essie's front door.

"Santos?" Essie whispered as she rose and headed cautiously to the door.

"No, Miss Essie," came the reply. "It's Hubert. Hubert Darby."

Essie froze in her tracks and looked back at Clara who motioned her to answer the door, indicating that she would remain where she sat and keep the baby occupied. Essie quickly moved to the door and opened it just a crack. Hubert Darby stood in the hallway. He was wearing a different Christmas vest from the last one she had seen. The light green paper face mask almost covered his blushing face.

"Hubert!" she cried. "What are you doing here? Happy Haven is under quarantine you know. Residents are all supposed to be in their rooms."

"Yes, Miss Essie," Hubert replied softly, his face turning even redder as he stared down at the carpet at his feet. "I came down to see you. I came down to see if you had opened my present." He said this last word so softly that Essie could barely hear him. She leaned out of her doorway over her walker, but kept the door itself closed so that Hubert could not see into her apartment. "Did you open my present, Miss Essie?" he asked again.

"Yes, I did, Hubert," she said, lifting her finger up and shaking it at Hubert. "You lied to me! You told me it was peanut brittle!"

Hubert's eyes bulged as Essie's finger closed in on his nose.

"I . . . I was afraid you might not open it, Miss Essie, if . . ."

"Hubert, that necklace is much too expensive for me to accept. It wouldn't be appropriate!" she cried. "Just a minute, I'll get it." She started to turn back into her living room.

"No, Miss Essie," exclaimed Hubert, following her through the door.

"Hubert, wait!" said Essie, turning around in an attempt to push the large man back into the hallway. "You can't come in here! The quarantine!" Unfortunately, Hubert had already seen Clara sitting serenely on Essie's sofa rocking baby Antonio–no face mask in sight.

"Hello, Hubert!" said Clara graciously to the man. Hubert stood dumbfounded just inside of Essie's front door. Essie looked back and forth from Hubert to Clara. "Essie, you might as well close the door before more people decide to join us." She gave Essie a little nod towards her front door. Essie gave a little grimace and rolled back and closed the door. Hubert moved towards Clara and the baby.

"That's a baby!" he said, pulling down his face mask and looking puzzled as he stared at Clara and then back again at Essie.

"We can explain, Hubert," said Essie, "would you like to have a seat?"

"Here, Hubert," said Clara, like a spider speaking to a fly, "sit here next to me. This is Antonio. Isn't he adorable?" Hubert carefully placed himself at the far end of Essie's small sofa. "He won't bite you, Hubert," said Clara. "Haven't you ever seen a newborn baby before?"

"No," replied Hubert, examining the infant with a mixture of wonder and fear. Then, a puzzled look covering his face, he looked over to Essie who had resumed her rocker. "Miss Essie? Why do you have a baby here?"

"I know it looks strange, Hubert," replied Essie, "but there really is a sensible reason."

"Essie's trying to track down his mother," said Clara. "She's missing!"

"The baby's mother? Do you know her?" asked Hubert, shaking his head in confusion. "What does Miss Violet say? Does she know that you have a baby in here?"

"Oh, no!" said Essie. "And Hubert, you can't tell her!"

"Oh, I won't, Miss Essie," said Hubert. "I'll do whatever you say, Miss Essie."

"How sweet!" declared Clara, looking at Hubert as he stared fondly at Essie and sighed. "Young love!"

"Clara, stop," said Essie. "Hubert, we're watching this baby for one of Happy Haven's kitchen workers . . . Maria Compton. She's disappeared. Her husband was killed in a car accident last night and we can't seem to locate her. It's a complex story, but it involves immigration . . . and we don't want to see this little one get deported or taken from his mother. He's part of the Happy Haven family and we all need to work together to find this child's mother and to protect him until we do. And, Hubert, that means keeping his existence a secret . . . especially from Violet!"

"Oh, Miss Essie!" declared Hubert. "I will keep your secret. I will help you protect the little baby." He bent in to the child and looked carefully at its face. "It's so little."

"He's only a few days old," replied Clara as Hubert showed interest in the child. "You can touch him, Hubert. He won't bite you." She held the little bundle out towards the big man in the red vest. Hubert lifted his hand with a delicacy totally unexpected for a man of his large frame and touched the baby's soft cheek.

"He's soft," said Hubert, breaking out into a warm smile.

"Most babies are," replied Clara, her face glowing as Hubert stared at the baby in her arms.

Essie watched the scene play out between Clara, Hubert, and baby Antonio. Eventually, she picked up the Kreigsted box on her end table. She gave a little cough to gain Hubert's attention.

"Hubert, since you're here, I can return this necklace to you." She reached over Clara to hand the box to Hubert, who waved it away and leaned back.

"No, Miss Essie!" he said, "I want you to have it."

"Hubert," Essie insisted, "I can't accept this from you. It's obviously a very expensive necklace." She opened the blue box and removed the golden necklace.

"I got it for you, Miss Essie," the large man continued.

"It's too expensive," said Essie. "Look!" She held the necklace up to the light for Hubert to see. As she dangled the sparkling object over Clara and towards Hubert, baby Antonio's eyes widened in apparent delight.

"Antonio likes the necklace, Essie," said Clara. "See it sparkle, Antonio!" She took the necklace from Essie and moved it around in front of the baby's face.

"I thought you would like it too, Miss Essie. You took it!" cried Hubert.

"You said it was peanut brittle," responded Essie, "I'd be happy to accept a box of peanut brittle from you, but not an expensive necklace like this. You should only give something like this to your wife or a member of your family."

Hubert's shoulders drooped and his head fell. He scratched his head and looked puzzled. Poor man! He obviously doesn't understand the niceties of gift exchange, thought Essie.

"I want to make you happy, Miss Essie. The baby likes the necklace," said Hubert forlornly, as he peeked up into Essie's face. "I want to make you happy like the baby. You are so wonderful . . . ."

"Thank you, Hubert," replied Essie. This was so much harder than she had expected. She surely didn't want to hurt the man's feelings, but she couldn't accept this present and he needed to understand why. Somehow she had to make him understand without hurting his feelings. "At least, Antonio can enjoy the necklace for a while." She smiled at Clara and Hubert as the three of them focused on the little boy as he waved his fists at the gleaming gold pendant swinging back and forth before his eyes. They all smiled and laughed warmly at the child. Antonio gurgled.

A sharp knock on the door was followed by a voice calling out, "Miss Essie, it's Violet Hendrickson! I need to speak to you!"

Oh no! thought Essie, Violet is at my front door and I have a room full of guests . . . and a baby during a quarantine! This is not good!

Essie quickly motioned for Clara to take Antonio and go to her bedroom. Clara rose, grabbed the baby, and walked quickly into Essie's back room. Essie then motioned Hubert to follow her. Hubert shook his head, but Essie nodded firmly, and Hubert shuffled rapidly behind Clara and disappeared. Essie then grabbed her walker and rolled to her door and opened it.

"Miss Hendrickson!" she cried, flinging the door open with feigned enthusiasm. "How nice to see you here. It's so boring just sitting here in my room all alone during this quarantine. It's wonderful just to see another human being for a change!" Too thick, Essie thought.

"Don't try that with me, Essie," replied Violet through her face mask. "I know you're up to something. I can hear you half the way down the hallway."

"Oh, sorry, Miss Violet!" replied Essie. "That was probably my television again. My hearing's not so good so I usually keep the volume pretty high. I'll watch that. I will."

Violet looked over Essie's head into her living room. Her eyes quickly scanned the area.

"You don't have any visitors?" she asked.

"Oh, no!" replied Essie. "I'd be much too frightened to have anyone over. Not with this horrible bug going around! I surely don't want to catch any virus!" She gave a nice fake cough in Violet's direction and the Director backed up a few feet.

"Humph!" responded Violet, "That's a good attitude. Everyone should remain in their rooms until the doctors tell us it's safe for residents to move about outside. It will protect us . . . I mean, you."

"Yes, indeed!" declared Essie, with a little fist pump. "I'm all for protecting us!"

Violet peered once more over Essie's head and apparently found her apartment satisfactorily empty. Then, turning abruptly on her heels, and without even a goodbye, she headed back down the hallway.

Chapter Twenty-Seven
"A baby is born with a need to be loved–and never outgrows it."
–Frank A. Clark

As soon as Violet had disappeared, Essie saw Santos quickly round the corner at the end of her hallway, his arms loaded with a large food tray and head in her direction. She held the door open for him as he entered and placed the heavy tray on Essie's kitchen counter.

"Miss Violet was here, Miss Essie?" he asked with trepidation.

"She was here, Santos," replied Essie, "but she didn't come in. I managed to stall her."

"Is baby with Miss Clara?" asked Santos. As he asked, Clara wandered into the living room with Antonio over her shoulder, followed by Hubert Darby.

"Madre de dios!" exclaimed Santos, "Senor Darby!"

"It's fine, Santos," replied Essie, her hand on the young man's shoulder, "Hubert is on our side . . . on Antonio's side."

Santos looked flustered and then relaxed noticeably.

"I am afraid all of Happy Haven soon know about Antonio, Miss Essie!" he said.

"Don't worry!" she replied. "He's among friends. He's in good hands." Clara and Hubert smiled at Santos, and Hubert patted Antonio's bottom with a chuckle.

"Very nice baby," he said. "I don't know much about babies, but this is a nice baby." He looked at Essie and then at the floor, immediately tongue-tied.

"I bring you and Miss Clara your supper, Miss Essie," said Santos, turning back to the tray and removing the lids from the various dishes. "I hope you like roast beef and carrots."

"That sounds delicious, Santos!" declared Clara, continuing to bounce Antonio. "Essie, what do you do about preparing those weird bottles for this little fellow?"

"Oh, we have that all worked out, Clara!" she replied.

"Si, Miss Clara," added Santos. "Miss Essie is very clever lady."

Essie and Santos remained in the kitchen taking the plates out and pouring glasses of water.

"Can I help?" asked Hubert, traipsing along behind Essie.

"Hubert, you sit down and we'll have you hold Antonio while Clara and I eat our dinners. Is that okay with you?" replied Essie.

"Oh, yes, Miss Essie," replied Hubert, shuffling over to the sofa and sitting on the end where he could rest his arm on the edge.

"Here you go," said Clara, rising and gently placing the baby in Hubert's arms. Essie and Clara picked up their prepared plates from the kitchen and joined Hubert around Essie's coffee table.

"Senor Hubert," said Santos, standing in front of the three of them, "do you want me to bring you dinner here too?"

"Oh, I don't want to impose on Essie," Hubert replied, blushing.

"Yes, Santos," ordered Essie. "Bring Hubert a plate too." Santos quickly headed out of the apartment, closing the door quietly behind him.

"We're all living dangerously," noted Clara as she speared a carrot. "Essie, you were amazing in fending off Violet. I could hear you from your bedroom. If anyone knew that three Happy Haven residents were sitting in your apartment together having dinner . . . and without face masks . . . during a quarantine . . . they would freak out!"

"Freak out! I like that!" repeated Hubert, nodding his head with a maniacal laugh, as he gently bounced Antonio in his lap.

"We surely don't want anyone freaking out!" added Essie, joining the laughter. At that, baby Antonio let out a loud cry. Essie held up her finger in a "shh" gesture to Hubert and Clara. "I'll go change his diapers," she said, rolling over to Hubert and grabbing the infant from Hubert's lap and placing him in her basket.

"Now I know what you've been hiding in that basket of yours, Miss Essie!" said Hubert merrily.

"It's very convenient," replied Essie, zipping through her bedroom door.

"Do you need help, Essie?" yelled Clara after her.

"No!" called back Essie, "you two just relax. Maybe you can think of some other places we might look for Maria."

Essie fiddled around with baby Antonio, changing his diapers and powdering his little bottom with some of her body powder. Antonio cooed and seemed to giggle when she lifted his rear end. She made sure she had plenty of infant-sized diapers that Fay had created out of her Reliables. Luckily, there was still a large stack of them above her commode. After being changed and rocked a bit, Antonio fell quickly asleep and Essie laid him down on the center of her bed. Then she wheeled herself back into the living room and resumed sitting in her lounge chair.

"So," she said to her new friends, "I just got him to sleep. Any ideas about where to look for Antonio's mother?"

"I told Hubert everything you and your friends have done to try to track Maria down, Essie," said Clara. "We both believe that someone needs to inform the police that she's missing."

"Yes," said Hubert. "Something bad may have happened to the baby's mother. The police can find her."

"I agree," said Essie, "but I don't think we . . . I mean . . . me or you, Clara or Hubert . . . should be the ones to contact the police. I think it should be Santos if anyone contacts them. I mean, Santos is the person Maria originally entrusted with her baby. He knows her the best. He has the most information about her."

"And," added Clara, "he can tell the police she's missing without mentioning any of the residents here at Happy Haven."

"I was thinking that too," said Essie. "If we report Maria to the police, they're going to wonder how we got involved and eventually it will come out that we've been keeping him here at Happy Haven . . . and that won't be good for any of us."

"Yes," said Hubert, nodding wisely. "Santos should call the police."

As if he heard them talking about him, Santos peeked his head in Essie's door and slipped in unannounced. He was holding a small food tray which he brought over to Hubert.

"Here you go, Senor Darby," he said. "Same as for ladies! You enjoy!" He removed the lid and Hubert dug into his supper enthusiastically. "Where is baby, Miss Essie?" asked the young worker, looking around.

"He's napping, Santos," replied Essie. "Don't worry. Santos, we all agree that it's time to report Maria missing. And we all agree that you should be the one to do it."

"Me?" replied Santos, backing up, a worried look on his face.

"Yes," she said. "We'll talk you through it. But, Santos, it really needs to come from you. If a Happy Haven resident reports her, the police are going to wonder why it's us. It makes sense that you would report her missing. You're the closest to her, now that her husband is . . . gone. But, Santos, I've been thinking about this. I don't know how you all feel about this, but I suggest that Santos only report Maria missing. I don't think he should mention the baby, because if he does, the police will surely want to know where the baby is, and then . . ."

"We'll have to tell them," said Hubert, finishing her statement. "That would not be good."

"They might take Antonio and put him in a . . . ." Clara began.

"Foster home," concluded Santos. "I do not want Antonio to go to foster home. Okay, Miss Essie. I call police, but I do not speak English so good . . ."

"You speak excellent English," said Essie.

"Very good English," added Clara.

"I completely understand you," concluded Hubert. Santos beamed as his three compatriots encouraged him and gave him the support he needed to make the important call. Essie picked up her telephone receiver and opened her directory to the page for local government offices. She quickly found the number again for the local police department and tapped in the numbers. When the operator answered, she handed the receiver to Santos.

"Hello," said Santos. "I have a friend who is missing. Can you help me find her?"

"One moment," replied the operator.

"She says 'one moment' and I wait," said Santos to the group. Soon, someone answered the call. Santos spoke.

"I have a friend who is missing," he said.

Essie and her two neighbors listened to Santos's end of the conversation. She was gratified that Santos built a good case for the police to begin searching for the young woman.

"I worry maybe Maria is hurt," Santos said to the officer. "Maria's husband, Gerald, he is very bad man. He hurt Maria. Gerald is in car accident last night. He is killed. I worry Maria may be hurt too. Si, Gerald Compton."

Santos was silent as he waited and then spoke again evidently in response to some new information from the police.

"Si, Senor," said Santos. "I do not understand all about the marriage and the law, but Maria is wife of Gerald. She has green card. No, she not return to her country! I worry something bad happen to Maria. Maybe husband hurt Maria bad before he is in car accident."

Santos listened again and Essie could see his face become increasingly agitated.

"No, Senor," said Santos, "I am only friend. Maria's relatives all in Mexico. No! It cannot be! Maria not leave here! Please help me find her!"

"Tell him she didn't have any money, so she couldn't afford to go back to Mexico," Essie whispered . "Tell him she couldn't drive."

"She not have money! She cannot drive!" he yelled into the phone. "Please help, Senor!" Santos listened again and then looked a little panicked.

"Me?" asked Santos. "A telephone number?" He looked around, confused.

"Tell him to call Happy Haven," said Essie.

"I work at Happy Haven," said Santos into the receiver. "You can call me here." He gave the officer the Happy Haven main number which Essie quickly wrote for him on a small notepad on her end table. "Gracias, Senor," said Santos, as the conversation concluded.

"That was good," said Essie. "Now maybe somebody will do something and find that poor young woman."

"I wouldn't count on it," added Clara from the sofa, "because in my experience there's not much the police can do in most missing persons' cases unless they find a body. And we aren't hoping for that!"

"Certainly not!" agreed Hubert next to her.

"No, please! No bodies!" said Santos aghast. As it appeared all three residents had finished their meals, Santos quickly gathered their trays and the tray toppers he'd left on Essie's kitchen counter and started to head out her door. Abruptly, he stepped back and slammed the door shut.

"Miss Essie," he whispered, "It's Miss Lorena! She come from room down in the hallway. She is on way to your room, Miss Essie!" He clutched the three dinner trays in apparent uncertainty as to what to do next.

"Loads of toads!" cried Essie, "Will we never get a moment of calm? Santos, you go on back to the kitchen. If Lorena asks you about all the trays, just say I was very hungry tonight. Hubert and Clara, go to the bedroom, you two! I never thought I'd make that suggestion to a couple here at Happy Haven!" Everyone jumped to their appointed locations and Essie reclined in her rocker and tried to adopt a relaxed posture.

Shortly, Lorena's friendly face appeared in her doorway.

"Miss Essie!" Lorena said in her slow, pleasant voice, "Now what mischief are you up to tonight?"

Chapter Twenty-Eight
"A baby is God's opinion that the world should go on."
—Carl Sandburg

"Lorena!" said Essie in a friendly greeting. She gave a little fake yawn as if she'd been dozing in her rocker.

"Sorry, honey," said Lorena, moving inside and closing the door. She immediately hustled over to the kitchen and removed the pill box from the cupboard above the sink. "Didn't mean to wake you."

"No, no!" replied Essie. "Just taking a little snooze. You know, to pep myself up!"

"You sure need a lot of pep for all that party plannin' you been doin', Miss Essie," said Lorena, gathering Essie's night time pills and filling her water glass. "How is that surprise comin' along?"

"Oh, just fine!" Essie lied. She had to search her brain to remember what sort of fanciful tale she had told Lorena last night. Oh, yes, she remembered. She'd told her she was planning a Christmas surprise party . . . or present . . . or something. It was a good thing she was so old and could always use her advanced age as an excuse for any memory problem she might have.

Lorena moved to Essie's chair.

"Here you go!" She handed her the handful of pills and then the glass of water. Essie downed the pills as quickly as she was capable of swallowing. "My Lord, you are whizzin' through them pills lately, Miss Essie! You used to hate takin' those big ones!"

"There's no sense in procrastinating," said Essie, attempting to move things along.

"Then, I'd best be gettin' your nightie so you don't procrastinate your bed time," said Lorena, heading for the bedroom.

"Oh, Lorena, no!" cried Essie, grabbing the aide's elbow. "I . . . I . . . I've decided not to get my pajamas on just yet."

"Lordy, Miss Essie," said Lorena, shaking her head and peering at Essie more carefully. "You been nippin' at the sherry?"

"The what?" cried Essie. "No! Of course not, Lorena. I just . . . I just thought I might take a walk a bit later. I can get my pajamas on myself. You don't need to come back."

"A walk?" exclaimed the rotund nurse. "You know HH is smack dab in the middle of a quar-an-tine, don't you? Just where's you planning on walkin'? You're not allowed out of your room!"

"We're not allowed to congregate in the major parts of the building. I was sort of thinking that I might like to take a . . . a walk . . . outside to get some . . . fresh air."

"Ha!" shrieked Lorena, "It's ten degrees below zero outside, Miss Essie! We're in the middle of a great big ol' snowstorm! You'd freeze your little ol' feathered hat right to your head!"

"I really need to get out," said Essie insistently. "I just feel claustrophobic in here."

"Better to be a claustro . . . whatever phobic . . . than a frozen icicle!" declared Lorena.

"I won't go far," continued Essie in her plea. Anything to keep Lorena from going in my bedroom and discovering Clara, Hubert, and baby Antonio. It would be easier to explain a penchant for winter walks than harboring residents and babies in my bedroom during a quarantine.

"I hope you change your mind," directed Lorena, shaking her finger in Essie's face. Essie merely smiled sweetly at her. Eventually, Lorena gathered up Essie's pill supplies and replaced them in the cupboard. "Okay, Missie, I'm goin' but I better not hear that they found your stone cold body out in the parking lot tomorrow mornin'!" She scowled at Essie and disappeared out her front door. You can't scare me, thought Essie.

Chapter Twenty-Nine

"I see something deeper, more infinite, more eternal than the ocean in the expression of the eyes of a little baby when it wakes in the morning and coos or laughs because it sees the sun shining on its cradle."
–Vincent van Gogh

After Lorena had gone, Essie gave the "all-clear" signal for Clara and Hubert who returned to the living room deep in conversation. Clara was laughing and giggling at Hubert's witticisms. Baby Antonio was sound asleep. Essie assured her two new friends that she could handle the baby through the night. Then they carefully sneaked out of the door and quietly returned to their own rooms.

Essie went into her bedroom and slowly readied herself for bed. Yes, it was much more difficult without Lorena's help, but she could do it. Taking care of Antonio had made her realize how truly capable she was . . . and getting her pajamas on was not really all that trying. She slipped out of her shoes and socks and placed them by her bed so they'd be easy to find in the morning. Then she took off her trousers and top . . . which were still clean . . . and set them on a chair by her closet. Quickly, she slipped on her pink nylon pj's from her top dresser drawer. After a quick trip to the potty and also the kitchen for a refill on the artificial formula, she wheeled back to her bedroom and traded places with her little buddy . . . putting Antonio in the basket and crawling into her bed.

"Oh, John," she said out loud to her husband . . . just in case he happened to be listening, "what a merry adventure I've gotten myself into now!" She wondered what John would think of her babysitting a newborn infant at her age . . . all by herself . . . well, almost all by herself. It's one thing to take care of a baby when you're young, but old people just don't have the stamina for it . . . at least not every single day. "I'll be so happy when we find Antonio's mother!"

Now that the police were on the lookout for Maria, maybe she would be located. Maybe they would even put an announcement on television about her being missing. Surely, someone would know something. And surely, she thought, I'll be out of the baby-sitting business! She glanced over to the side of her bed where the baby was sleeping comfortably in her walker basket. I hope I'll be out of the baby-sitting business! This thought was firmly in her mind as she drifted off to sleep.

She slept more soundly than she had in ages. It was probably all that activity and exercise, she thought. An invigorating stretch moved from the tips of her fingers to the tips of her toes. A beam of light shot across her bedspread, forcing her to turn her head to her window. Sunbeams were fighting to make their way through the spaces between her blinds. She could hear a few cars outside, cars actually speeding rather rapidly down the street in front of Happy Haven. The only sound that seemed even vaguely reminiscent of the previous night's storm was a sporadic slushing noise when a car wheel splattered wet snow against the curb. She rolled over to where her walker stood, beside her bed and bent over to peek at baby Antonio in his basket.

He wasn't there. No. That couldn't be right. He was a baby. He couldn't get up and walk away. Had she put him to sleep somewhere else and forgotten about it? Quickly, she rose and wheeled her walker into the bathroom where she had placed the baby the other morning when DeeDee came to get her ready. There was no sign of the baby. Oh, no! Where could he be? She rolled herself quickly to the living room and looked around, but it was horrifically obvious that the baby . . . the sweet little boy she had promised to care for while they tried to find his missing mother . . . was missing himself!

Now, stop, Essie! she said to herself. There must be an explanation. Someone must have taken him. Someone who must have known he was here and was so quiet they didn't even wake me! Me! she thought. One of the lightest sleepers in the world. Panic rose in her heart as she tried desperately to determine what had happened to the baby. She'd have to go look for him.

She called the main desk. Phyllis was not yet on duty and one of the night workers answered.

"Can you connect me to the kitchen?" she asked, trying to make her voice sound calm although she felt increasingly horrible.

"The kitchen?" the woman asked.

"Yes, please," said Essie. Soon, an older woman answered.

"Yes, hello?" said the woman.

"Hello," replied Essie. "Is Santos there?"

"He no here now," said the woman. "Just me."

"When will he be there?" asked Essie, hope draining away.

The woman repeated, "Just me. No Santos."

"Thank you," said Essie and quietly replaced the receiver. Her heart was beating ferociously. She could not calm her body or her mind. She rolled herself back into her bedroom and dressed in her clothes from yesterday as quickly as she could. Then, she pushed herself to her front room and pulled her winter coat and hat from her front closet. She quickly dressed for the cold. At least, the storm had subsided. She moved to her front door, determined to go out looking for Santos. If he didn't know where Antonio was, no one would.

When she opened the door, Santos was standing in the hallway, hand up ready to open her door knob. Beside him stood a young woman, whom Essie immediately recognized as Maria Valdez Compton. She was holding Antonio in her arms.

"Antonio!" cried Essie, reaching out over her walker to touch the young child. A tear gushed from her eye and she wiped it away with her coat sleeve. "I thought someone kidnapped him!" she cried to them, as more tears poured forth.

"No, Miss Essie!" whispered Santos, happily. "Antonio is fine! Maria is fine! We come in and explain!"

"Of course, of course!" she replied and ushered them into her living room.

"Miss Essie, this Maria," said Santos, introducing the two women. Essie pulled Maria to her chest and hugged her and the little baby as a unit. It was a long hug. She did not want to let them go. Eventually, they all removed their winter coats and sat down, with baby Antonio on his mother's lap.

"First, Miss Essie," said Santos, "I am so very sorry, I take Antonio from you late late at night. Maria come back late . . . very late. She wants to see baby so bad. I not want to wake you up. You sleep, Miss Essie. So, I take Antonio and give him to Maria. I think I get back here before you wake up. But, no! You wake up very early, Miss Essie!"

"Yes, I do, young man!" said Essie, shaking her finger at Santos. "And finding that baby gone about gave me heart failure! That's not a good thing at my age!"

"I so sorry, Miss Essie," said Maria in a soft, gentle voice. "Santos tell me how wonderful you be to my baby. I want to say thank you."

"There's no need for that, my dear," said Essie to the young woman on her sofa. "Just be a good mother to that little boy. That's the only thanks I want."

"Si," replied Maria and squeezed her child close to her breast.

"Now, Santos . . . and Maria," Essie said, "can I get an explanation of what happened? Where have you been all this time, Maria?"

"Is like you say, Miss Essie," said Santos, quickly. "Maria, she fall. Maria, Gerald, they have big fight."

"Si," agreed Maria, "he no want me keep baby. He say he can give baby away because he is husband. I no think that is American way, but I not know."

"Horrible!" cried Essie. "What I disgusting man! Excuse me, Maria. I know he was your husband, but . . ."

"Is all right," responded Maria. "Gerald very different in Mexico. We get married. We come America. Then Gerald, he is very mean. I not know why."

"So what happened after the fight?" asked Essie.

"I run from house," said Maria. "Gerald, he follow me. He get in car. He yell at me. He yell he get me, he kill me. I run very fast, but I hear Gerald car come after me, very fast. I run away into woods. I no hear car. I run more into woods, but I trip and fall. No remember then."

"A very nice man, Senor Shepherd, he . . . how you say . . .he rescató . . . rescued . . . Maria," said Santos.

"Si," added Maria, "he take me to hospital."

"Why didn't you call Santos?" asked Essie.

"I call Santos right away," she said, looking at Santos, puzzled.

"Maria was . . . inconsciente . . . unconscious until yesterday," he explained.

"Si," said Maria, "I not know many hours go by. When I wake up, I worry much because Santos take care of Antonio. I worry Santos not know how care baby."

"You needn't have worried," said Essie to Maria in a tender, reassuring voice and a gentle hand on her arm. "Santos is a very kind man."

"Si," said Maria, blushing. Blushing, Essie thought to herself. Maybe Clara is on to something. Maybe there is a budding romance between these two. How sweet!

A soft knock on the door.

All three froze and glanced at the baby.

"It's us, Essie," said Clara's voice. "Me and Hubert."

"Just a minute," replied Essie as she rose to answer her door.

"No one saw you, did they?" Essie asked. They both shook their heads and quickly discarded their face masks. When Clara and Hubert entered, they both beamed when they saw Maria with her baby. They went over and respectfully looked on as Essie and Santos explained how Maria had been located.

Another knock on the door caused all of the people in the room to freeze again, but the sudden fear changed to relief, when Opal, Marjorie, and Fay entered, all dropping their paper masks at the door.

"A little bird told us there was a reunion going on down here!" cried Marjorie, rolling excitedly over to the group surrounding Antonio and his young mother. Opal and Fay quickly joined her. Essie and Santos delighted in repeating the happy story of how they located Antonio's mother.

"How wonderful! You're all here! And none of you got caught!" said Essie to the entire group. "This is surely the best Christmas present ever!"

Chapter Thirty
"When the first baby laughed for the first time, the laugh broke into a thousand pieces and they all went skipping about."
James Matthew Barrie

The tall spruce was gleaming as it seemed to look down in pride at the large group gathered beneath its branches in the Happy Haven family room. On the far end of the room, a chorus of young children all decked out in red and white choir robes, holding hymnals, were serenading the residents. Most all of the residents were seated on sofas and chairs and many additional folding chairs that had been set up to accommodate the overflow crowd. Indeed, it was an overflow crowd, as many residents had invited family members to join them for the concert that had been postponed for days due to a bad stomach virus and a raging snowstorm. Both had now passed. Behind the seated residents, many staff members stood, also enjoying the Christmas music. The air was filled with a wonderful holiday aroma that Essie now knew was composed of traditional frankincense and myrrh.

Essie herself was in the last row of folding chairs near the tree. On her right sat her three children—Prudence, Kurt, and Claudia. On her left, sat her three best friends—Opal, Marjorie, and Fay. Her friends had by now heard all the details about the discovery of Antonio's mother.

"Oh, this takes me back to my days of teaching elementary school!" whispered Marjorie. She sighed as several of the smallest carolers came forward and sang solos. "Aren't they adorable?"

"Not as adorable as Antonio," said Opal, leaning in to her friend.

"Of course not!" agreed Marjorie. "Oh, I miss him!"

Fay and Essie smiled at their two friends and all four women beamed at each other in a spirit of solidarity.

"Thank you, dear friends," whispered Essie, when the program had ended and the audience members began to chat and move around, "thank you, all, for your help."

She reached over and squeezed their hands. Then, realizing that they were ignoring Essie's children, the friends concluded their private discussion and focused their attention on Essie's family.

"It's wonderful that the quarantine and the snowstorm are over just in time for Christmas," said Opal to Essie's children.

"And it's wonderful that the children's choir was able to reschedule to perform for us at the last moment! It just wouldn't be Christmas without them!" added Marjorie. Prudence, Claudia, and Kurt agreed and smiled warmly at Essie's three friends.

A man in the row directly in front of them turned around.

"Hello, Miss Essie," said Hubert Darby. "Merry Christmas," he said to all of Essie's family.

"Hello, Hubert," replied Essie. She introduced the man to her children. The woman sitting next to Hubert also turned around and greeted Essie and her children.

"Hello, Essie," said Clara. "Merry Christmas to you." Essie's children greeted Clara. Opal, Marjorie, and Fay looked at Clara knowingly and each glanced back at Essie.

"You all may not know," whispered Essie to her friends, "but my next door neighbor, Clara, is a former NICU nurse and knows a lot about taking care of infants." She gave Clara a nod. Opal, Marjorie, and Fay all bent forward and each gave Clara a warm hug.

Essie felt a soft tap on her shoulder. She turned and found herself looking up at Santos. Maria was standing beside him, holding Antonio in her arms.

"Merry Christmas, Miss Essie," he said.

"Oh, Santos, Merry Christmas," said Essie, and quickly added, "I'd like you to meet my children—Prudence, Claudia, and Kurt. I'm so delighted they were all able to come and enjoy this concert with us."

Essie's children greeted Santos, whom Essie introduced as her favorite waiter. They informed him that they were taking Essie out to dinner after the concert.

"Um, Miss Essie," said Santos, awkwardly, "this is . . . . uh . . . Maria and her son Antonio. She work in kitchen with Santos." Santos was not a good liar, but Essie appreciated his efforts.

"Is very Merry Christmas for Maria and Antonio," continued Santos. "Immigration Office says it not deport Maria. Says Maria and baby both licitó . . . how you say? Legal. Can stay in America!"

"That's wonderful, Santos!" exclaimed Essie.

"I go stay at Maria's apartment," Santos said. "I help Maria with baby."

"Very happy," said Maria. She looked adoringly at Santos.

Essie beamed at them and reached out for baby Antonio.

"Could I hold him?" she asked Maria. Maria smiled and handed the child down to Essie. Almost immediately, Essie's friends noticed the baby's presence and they all moved in around her closer to see him. Prudence, Claudia, and Kurt stood dumbfounded nearby as the group of elderly residents focused completely on one small, totally unknown–to Essie's children, at least–child.

"Hello, Antonio," said Essie. "Aren't you a little charmer? I doubt that the other residents will be able to resist you. We don't see many newborn infants here."

"Is okay," said Maria to Essie. "Antonio is Happy Haven resident too."

"He certainly is," agreed Essie, as a crowd of residents . . . even those who had no idea who he was . . . had formed around the little infant. Essie's children smiled from the sidelines.

"Hey, it's a baby!" cried one of the young carolers and a whole pack of youngsters quickly encircled Essie and the infant. "Can I touch him?" asked one little girl.

"Me too!" chimed in another girl. Soon all the children were stretching out their hands to touch the baby.

"I think you all had better just look at him," suggested their choir director behind the excited group of carolers. "Babies are very delicate." The children instantly calmed and watched the infant from a respectful distance. Many got on their knees so they could touch the baby's feet.

Across the room, Essie noticed a tall, older man come through the front door. He was wearing a long overcoat and snow boots. He had a full head of snow white hair and matching full white beard. Hmm, she thought. Maybe, he's going to play Santa Claus! That would be perfect! The man spoke to Phyllis at the front desk. Phyllis pointed towards the crowd and the man headed in their direction. When he arrived, he stopped and beamed at the infant in Essie's arms. Then his eyes scanned the crowd until they landed, a bit uncertainly, on Maria, standing behind Essie, next to Santos.

"Ms. Compton?" he asked Maria. "I'm delighted to see you up and about. The hospital told me where to find you. I'm Nick Shepherd. I . . . ."

"Oh!" cried Maria, with a look of sudden recognition on her face. She rushed to the large man and wrapped her small arms around him. She had to stand on her tiptoes and she could barely reach from one of his arms to another, let alone behind the large man's back. "Mr. Shepherd! Of course! Thank you!"

Essie, Santos, and the few other residents who were aware of Maria's recent trauma looked curiously at the young Hispanic woman and the rough-hewn older gentleman. Maria broke her hold of Nicholas Shepherd and turned back to the group.

"Senor Shepherd," she explained, "is person who found me when I fall other day. He bring me to hospital. He save my life . . . ." She looked up–way up–into the face of the stranger. His cheeks–noticeably red from the cold outdoor weather–gave him a cheery, dimpled look. He smiled down at the young woman.

"It's wonderful seeing you up and around, young lady!" said Shepherd. "No one should be stuck in a hospital during Christmas." He laughed heartily. It sounded like "ho-ho-ho" to Essie as she looked the huge man up and down.

"Gracias, Senor Shepherd," Maria repeated sincerely. "Thank you, so much!" She gave him another hug. As Maria and Shepherd began to tell the group about their adventure, the group of residents and children gathered around the unlikely pair. Essie handed the baby to Marjorie and moved out of the center of attention. She turned around to see Hubert Darby moving closer to her. He held the blue Kreigsted box in his hands.

Oh, no, she moaned to herself. I thought I'd convinced him to forget about giving me that necklace. Now, what does he want?

Hubert came up to Essie and held the box before him.

"Miss Essie," he said. "About the necklace . . . ."

"Hubert," she replied, "I told you I can't accept that necklace. It's just not appropriate."

"I know, Miss Essie," continued Hubert, "but do you think it would be appropriate for me to give the necklace to baby Antonio?"

"What?" she asked. "What would a baby do with an expensive piece of jewelry?"

"He likes it, Essie. Remember? In your living room? I think he liked the way the gold sparkled," said Hubert, and then when Essie looked shocked, Hubert Darby laughed. He had a very nice, warm laugh, thought Essie. "I'm teasing you, Miss Essie. I'm not teasing about giving the necklace to Antonio though. Antonio has had a very difficult start, I'm thinking. His mother is now a widow and will need help to care for him. If you don't want the necklace, then I would like to give it to him. I don't want to return it to the store. I don't need the money. I have more than I need. His mother may keep it for his future or sell it to help cover her expenses."

"That's very generous of you, Hubert! Maria will need money now that she has a baby to support all by herself. You are a wonderful man," replied Essie. "Oh, my mud pie! And I hadn't even thought about how she would be able to pay for her recent hospital stay. She's only a kitchen worker. Hospital bills can be horrific!"

Nicholas Shepherd evidently heard this discussion between Essie and Hubert and had left the group surrounding the baby to join them.

"I heard you mention Maria's hospital bills," he whispered to Essie and Hubert. "You don't need to worry. I took care of her bills."

"But, Mr. Shepherd," argued Essie, "you don't even know Maria. Why would you do such a thing?"

"Let's just say I was struck with the Christmas spirit," he said, with a mischievous smile and a jiggle of his large stomach. Then he walked around behind them as he took a good long look at the Happy Haven tree and its decorations. He appeared especially smitten with the little train at the tree's base, and gave the tiny conductor a jaunty salute. Essie glanced back to look at the baby for a moment, and when she turned around to see where Nicholas Shepherd had gone, he was nowhere to be seen.

"Where did Mr. Shepherd go?" Essie asked Hubert. Hubert looked around and shrugged. Essie and Hubert rejoined the group of their friends and family gathered around the little infant now back in his mother's arms. Essie looked over at Hubert at her side and grabbed his hand and gave it a little squeeze. Hubert blushed a fire-engine red, looked at the ground, and rocked back and forth on his feet.

"Oh, Miss Essie!" he blubbered. The choir director had one more number for the group and directed the carolers to begin singing "Oh Come All Ye Faithful." As the sweet young voices echoed through the halls of Happy Haven, all of the residents and their families joined in, until finally everyone was singing the hymn. The music swelled until it sounded like a throng of angels was serenading one tiny little papoose who was in the center of it all.

THE END

ABOUR THE AUTHOR

Patricia Rockwell is the author of two cozy mystery series. PAPOOSED is the second in her Essie Cobb senior sleuth mysteries. The first, BINGOED, introduced Essie and her gang of amateur detective friends who live in the Happy Haven Assisted Living Facility. The group attempt to find out what has caused a fellow resident to collapse and fall into a coma after he wins a dollar playing Bingo. Their efforts are rewarded with a series of merry adventures, just as in PAPOOSED.

Rockwell also writes the Pamela Barnes acoustic mystery series, which follows the psychologist and acoustics expert as she assists local police in solving various crimes with sound clues. In the first of these, SOUNDS OF MURDER, Pamela discovers an accidentally-made audio recording of a strangling death and uses her knowledge of sound to determine the identity of the killer. The second book, FM FOR MURDER, presents Pamela with an intriguing case. A local disc jockey is shot to death on-air. No one sees the killer but many listeners hear the crime unfold. Pamela uses the radio station's recording to help the police track down the wily murderer. In the third of the series, VOICE MAIL MURDER, Pamela helps in an investigation of the local university football coach's murder. The man is found stabbed to death in a seedy motel. The only clue is his cell phone which contains voice mail messages from three unknown women. Pamela uses her knowledge of the sound of the human voice to help the police solve this mysterious case.

All of Rockwell's books are available in both paperback and e-book format on Amazon and other sites. You can read more about this author and her work on the publisher's website: www.cozycatpress.com.

Made in the
USA
Monee, IL

15825710R00159